# Nor the Moon Shall See Them.

Julie Buckingham.

# PRELUDE

He sat on his plush white sofa, his real gold phone carefully held with soft manicured fingers to his ear demanding crisply, in English: "Are we ready to put my new plan into action?"

He received a crackly affirmative on the end of his line, which made him smile deviously.

"You've taken care of everything your end of the world? It is so – I can't wait to receive the goods! She'll arrive tomorrow? Ah! That makes me very pleased! May Allah be with you!"

Something else was said, or asked, and the man on the gold phone narrowed his eyes. "I take no notice of them!" He snarled. "Our police officers like my pay, but our laws are still strict. My crimes stay overlooked, and I keep it that way! Whoever is making inquiries into my affairs will pay for it with their lives if they come here! The police in England do not bother me unless they get too close! I am safe! Tell me more about this 'inquiring' Englishman'? Why should he show such an interest in me? What is his name?"

The man listened, sharp-eyed, as further explanations followed. He grinned wickedly. "Ah, so...because of that, eh? I will not change my plans now. Nor must you! He must have bribed someone in higher office to learn such scant information! I'm not worried! If this agent shows up in my country I'll have one of my men follow him! He'll wish he'd never arrived here – I'll make it difficult for him! He can be killed if necessary!"

"Yes, you may have to!" The voice the other end was acerbic and dry.

"No worries my friend. We'll continue with our plan. Goodbye!"

# LONDON. TWO HOURS BEFORE MIDNIGHT, FRIDAY, JULY 2017

Guys and girls were dancing on the disco floor, stomping and stumbling over each other's feet to the sound of a 90's song, singing along with it. The dance area was packed. Lights pulsated and flickered around the lit-up floor to the beat of the music, and colored pretend smoke swirled from the D J's corner, creating a surreal, ethereal effect. Many people were dancing in front of the DJ on a raised dais, especially created for those who wanted to stay separate from the main crowd and gyrate close to the hypnotic beat of the music he'd chosen.

Two girls at the back of the dance floor, both long-legged, long-haired blondes, were trying to communicate with each other. With the music so loud this was almost impossible in the heady, sweat-soaked atmosphere. The taller girl of the two, swished around in an expensive, bare-backed gold dress, and false eyelashes with gold glitter spattered on them.

"What's your name?" She shouted to the other girl.

"What's that you say?" The shorter girl wore a black strapless dress and flat, pointed shoes. Her long tangled hair had been pinned back to one side by an elaborately sparkling hair grip, eclipsing the curve of her clear-cut jawbone and pointed chin. She wore no make-up and didn't need to.

"What-is-your-name?" Elucidated the golden dressed girl, stopping still for a moment to wait for the other's reply.

"It's Fran! What's yours?"

"I'm Leigh!"

"Hi Leigh!"

"Hi Fran!"

They grinned like conspirators now they knew each other's names.

Fran's large green eyes began swerving around as if she was looking for someone. "Where's he gone?"

"Who? That man who was dancing with us? Is he your boyfriend?"

"What? No, he's not! I think he's gone to the bar."

Leigh only just heard Fran's voice above the beat of the noisy music.

"Yeah – for a drink!" Leigh shouted back.

Fran's eyes skewered the dance floor, searching, she grinned impishly clutching her new friend's arm. "There he is..., he's back! He's looking for us!" She pointed to the front of the dance floor where there was a gap in the crowd.

Leigh casually waved the man over. Grinning, he danced his way towards them to the music's beat, feinting from side to side like a drunk cobra swaying in its basket. He had an attractive shaved head and a charming man-about-town smile, and wore cool, casual modern clothes that suited his athletic figure. He looked like a man determined to dance the night away.

The girls giggled at his return and at his concentrated movements, both unsure whether he was drunk or not.

They both welcomed him back with eager, roguish expressions as they flirted around him, flattered by his company.

"He's good-looking!" Leigh approved, shouting hotly in Fran's ear. Fran nodded and gave an appreciative wolf-whistle, which no one heard in the noisy night club.

Fran yelled back to Leigh: "Let's find out his name?"

Being friendly and tipsy, they crowded around the man, bellowing and gesturing familiarly as if they'd known him a long time: "Hey! What's your name?"

"Karl." He shouted back, grinning at their interest in him.

He didn't ask about them! Leigh frowned, vaguely disappointed. Maybe he wasn't so interested in them as she'd supposed; he might fancy pretty Fran more than her! She shrugged. She didn't care!

It was obvious the man was enjoying their company. He linked arms around both girls, encouraging them to move with him. Awkwardly, they swayed in a threesome upon the crowded floor, trying to jig in sync with the music. Other people were doing the same, and it was a tangle of hot arms, legs and swirling bodies jiving madly to the pulsating beat, their body's sweat and smells poring off them, uncaring of the airless heat that enveloped them as stuffy as hell.

Everyone was happy doing their thing.

The trio were so enjoying themselves, like others, they were unaware they were being watched by three pairs of impatient eyes...

After ten minutes of breathless non-stop dancing Fran shouted in her new friend's ear: "Going to the loo, okay?"

"Okay!" Leigh continued to pounce around with the man called Karl, until he noticed his mobile light up. He caught Leigh's eye and tapped his mobile with a silent shrug, then made a pouring gesture at his throat, making signs he was leaving to go towards the crowded bar and get another drink.

Leigh nodded as he elbowed through the crowd towards the busy, neon-lit bar on the other side of the club, squinting at his text message under the low-key lighting.

Left to her own devices Leigh carried on dancing. She was soon joined by a slim, tallish girl, who had highlights in her blond-brown plaits. They ran from her crown down either side of her striking, elaborately made-up face. She reminded Leigh of an alert fawn. She had on a shiny beige top that tied under her breasts, and wore a short, split-leg, black leather skirt. They pounded the floor together within the space they had with friendly grins.

The new girl was doing a kind of arm-throwing jig,

where one hand came up and one arm went down, whilst she jumped from side to side. Leigh copied her, trying to keep up and master the crazy steps!

She bellowed. "This is fun!"

Abruptly, the girl spoke loudly to Leigh. "Phew! Bloody hot, isn't it? Do you like Tequila?"

"Um, not sure..."

"I've got loads of Tequila over at the bar, can't wait to drink it! Would you like to try some? Come with me – meet my two friends!"

Sweaty and flushed with movement, and the lively ambiance of the nightclub, Leigh's relaxed mind held no warnings, and she nodded her consent freely. The girl took hold of Leigh's hot hand and propelled the teen slowly through the dense crowd to the packed bar area, looking for her 'friends'.

Leigh followed willingly enough, trying not to tread on handbags and toes. She passed their dance-partner Karl, not aware he stood watching her among the crowd packed tightly around the bar. Frowning, he wondered where she was going with this new girl? He glanced towards the spot where the other girl Fran, had been dancing. Piqued he couldn't spot her, he shrugged his well-built shoulders and stayed where he was, looking worried...

Leigh's new friend, bull-dozing her way through the dense crowd, reached her destination, where a boy with heavy glasses, and a moody-looking dark-haired girl were silently sipping their drinks, sprawling indifferently against the busy bar's high counter.

The girl with blond highlights and plaited hair roughly pulled the boy's ear down to yell into it, and his eyes swiveled to Leigh without much interest. The other dark-haired girl looked bored and pensive, and barely took any notice of their new arrival, swigging her coke quickly.

A plastic glass was shoved into Leigh's receptive hand. Thirstily she gulped the Tequila, which was so strong it made her blue eyes sting.

The packed crowd near her, drinking solidly, watched

the wild antics of the uninhibited figures on the dance floor. The heat became unbearable as the music changed tempo to a harsh, blaring, screaming beat. Leigh became aware of it and began to feel sick. Her temples throbbed, she swayed, overcome with a strange dizziness.

"Gotta sit down! What's wrong with me?" She gasped. She sat heavily on the bottom of some nearby steps, numb and out of sorts.

The steps seemed to move under her, and the dance floor blurred and swam eerily before her eyes. She blinked, trying to focus.

The boy's face appeared enquiringly in front of her, focusing on her weakened condition with a kind of reserved academic interest. He still looked grim. She thought his glasses were misting up and she giggled feebly at this lanky comedian whose careful, watchful eyes behind his thick frames studied her – as if she was a lab experiment – with such thoughtful intent.

"Enjoying it? Have some more Tequila!" Another full plastic glass was placed in her hand. She shook her head – or tried to. Her eyes blurred. She said, "I feel faint. What's happening to me?"

The three of them, including the tall girl with the sandy plaits, were peering and probing inside her unzipped handbag. Why the hell were they rummaging in her bag? Concerned, Leigh tried to reach up and grab it back, instantly dropping her plastic glass on the floor which spilled over her shiny gold dress! To her stupefied surprise, she found the handbag snatch too much of an effort, and had to give up her urgent quest to get it back.

# LONDON, FRIDAY, LATE EVENING. THE KIDNAP

Someone grabbed Leigh's arm. Owlishly, the girl found herself squinting up at new friend Fran's pretty, puzzled face.

"You okay?" Fran asked loudly, concerned.

Leigh shook her head briskly, then wished she hadn't.

The boy with glasses pushed Fran away from Leigh. "She's had too much –" He mimed a drinking gesture with his hand. "We are taking her home!"

Fran did not like being pushed, and she didn't like the boy. His cold eyes behind his chunky, wedged-shaped glasses made her feel uneasy.

She shouted back: "I'm not happy with this... Are you her friends?"

"Friends...? Yeah, course! Move out the way can you? We need to get through!"

The boy jerkily dragged Leigh's placid arm around his neck and began to steer her away, whilst the other two girls silently followed, twisting as fast as they could through the dense crowd towards one of the exits, ignoring Fran.

Fran bellowed after them, "Hey, she liked it here! Where are you taking her?"

The trio didn't answer.

The evening having fallen flat, Fran squirmed her way back to her dance spot, grateful to see that Karl had returned. He looked as hot as she was, and his eyes were anxiously searching around the dance floor.

He looked startled when Fran skipped up to him and exclaimed: "Leigh's gone!"

He raised his eyebrows. "Who's Leigh?"

"My friend, the one you were jigging about with!"

6

Fran didn't wait for his reaction, acting on impulse, she grabbed his hand and signalled he should follow her.

Intrigued, he did so. At the exit door the security guard waved them out. They could still hear the ear-splitting blasts of popular chart music bursting out noisily from the club's open doors. It's tempo was warming up to a higher pitch for the feverish, dense, swaying crowd tucked inside!

The late evening air felt clammy, only a shade cooler than inside the nightclub, but it was still a welcome relief to be out in the open, away from packed, jostling arms. There were latecomers queuing at the side of the building to get in, but not many at the nightclub exit where they stood – apart from a guy swaying drunkenly who'd been sick on the pavement.

Fran immediately saw a rough-looking black Mazda with engine idling parked outside the club's doors. A helpless, disorientated Leigh had her hands tied up, and was being dragged into the rusty heap of a car by the group Fran had last spoken to.

Something was very wrong here, Fran thought!

Not stopping to think about her own safety, Fran didn't hesitate but charged forward, yelling: "Hey, you guy's? This isn't right! What are you doing with her? Why is she tied up?"

A knife flashed in the dark-haired girls hand as she raised it towards Fran's startled face. There was a vice-like grip on Fran's arm, and the boy hissed: "If you don't want Jaz to cut you, get in – NOW!"

It was an order the shocked girl could only obey.

Once she was shoved into the car at knife-point, so quick she could hardly think, the boy ordered tersely to the girl with plaits: "Move it, Sal, for bloody hell's sake – GO!"

Their dancing partner Karl, had witnessed this astounding incident. Now he moved towards the roaring car just as the girl with plaits accelerated off at high speed, carrying its two prisoners. The dark, grubby, old model Mazda was screeching down the road, and turning right even before he could switch his mobile on to make a call.

## LONDON BLUES. FOUR HOURS BEFORE THE KIDNAP, FRIDAY

Special police operator Karl Silverman, medium height, handsome and athletic-looking, jauntily bounded the ten steps up to Tanja Kovacevic's apartment, wearing casual evening dress of dark drainpipe jeans, and a smart polo shirt that showed up his muscled shoulders. Printed upon his bare right forearm, a decorated laurel-leaf navy-colored tattoo read "Watch me!"

He sported a shaved head with high cheekbones molded on a strong, tanned, intelligent face, framed by a short, sculptured chestnut beard that allowed a glimpse of the determined contours of his firm, no-nonsense jaw-line, and bright, oak-brown eyes. An old knife scar faintly puckered the left side of his mouth, due to one of the dangerous missions his elite department, CIUSO had sent him on. His department was known as 'the den', but officially called Criminal Intelligence Unit Special Operations.

Karl had successfully obtained Tanja's apartment for her and her young child after a relentless property search. He was late arriving, due to a night assignment he'd been ordered to work on, urgently assembled by 'the den'. Adrenaline surged in his body, already, he was looking forward to this new case, CIUSO had insight to it and suspected a sudden kidnap!

Tanja's small apartment was in a block of five, recently renovated outlets that the council had made habitable for those on low incomes. Young, ex-schoolteacher Tanja, bringing up her small child born in Croatia, with Karl's help in securing a British flat for her, had legally arrived in

England, and managed to get a job serving in a local coffee shop. Her English was good: she'd taught it at the school she'd once worked at in her own country. She could pay the London rent herself now, even though Karl had helped subsidize her at first.

Karl latch-keyed door number five with his key, which Tanja had entrusted him with, and entered the small hallway.

"Hi, Tanja, its me!"

"I'm busy in the kitchen!" Her voice sounded cross.

She did not rush to greet him as she usually did. She scowled tensely when he walked in, and looked in a bad mood.

"Hello – what's up?"

"I thought you'd come earlier than this! Its gone seven and I've sent Kimmi to bed! She was so looking forward to seeing you again!"

"I'm really sorry, I should have phoned. I've been busy rearranging my work schedules: I'm off on a night job, minding a rich banker's daughter – which may involve a surprise kidnap! You know how hectic my life is!"

"Oh, I do – you're damned job! A possible kidnap, huh? Why do you tell me this? Do I really need to know!"

"Yeah, I tell you because you're good at keeping things to yourself, and I need someone to talk to sometimes! Blow off steam! I thought you understood that?"

"Oh I do, only too well! You're off again, leaving me seething because you've only just got here!"

"Tanja, I didn't mean to upset you –!"

"Oh no? Well, you have! I'm pissed off with it! I thought you looked smart; all dressed-up for another assignment? It scares me! Your work is damn dangerous, I care you'll get hurt!"

"It's sweet of you to worry about me!"

"Only because you've looked after me, a dumb, frightened waif from a Croatian women's refuge, with a young kid in tow! That was ages ago now! I don't know why you bothered with us! I can't figure why you brought me here if you don't want me! Am I not sexy enough? Did you feel sorry for me – is that it? Are you a man, or a mouse?"

"Steady, what's brought this on? I'm –"

She didn't pause in her tirade, but went on relentlessly. "You look the type of man women confide in, tell their secrets too! I certainly did! But I don't understand you; you must have thousands of girl-friends in every country you've been assigned to! I really thought you'd care about us, but you don't seem keen now you've sussed what a bored, fretful, disgruntled, dissatisfied, moaning hag I've become! I need to be loved by someone – haven't you realized that, or are you stupid?"

"Whoa! You're coming on strong! Why haven't you mentioned all this before? You have an admirer! Kostas Barrado, the coffee-shop owner where you work! I didn't want to interfere in your love life if there's any romance happening between the pair of you!"

"Kostas works long hours, like you, his flat above his shop is bigger than this one! We've been stuck here nearly a year, and it's getting too small for us! I would prefer it if you were a home-lover, working nine to five, not a he-man traveling the world with guns flaring, fighting bad men! What did you see in me when you brought us here? Am I so pathetic that you scorn me when I need you?"

"Try not to get so heated, Tanja, Kimmi's asleep... She'll hear you! I had no idea you felt so deeply about this! I'm fond of both of you, but my job comes first – women second – as much as I like them! I can't afford to love you as you want me to. I can't be tied. I'm afraid I don't want you and Kimmi to be in any danger from my job!"

"You afraid? Huh, you don't know what real fear is, even though you face it twenty times a day! It's the loneliness, the need, dark nights and empty days... My terrible existence before you came along and rescued us warps me, even now! I've turned into a bitchy shrew who'll always nag you. Hear me before I go crazy – I want you to become my partner!"

"I know, I hear you...! I'm sorry, it wouldn't work out! Look how dissatisfied you are now! We would row and bicker over my job! If I said 'I love you' it wouldn't be enough! You'd still resent what I do for a living!"

"You held me and cuddled me when you found us, and said: 'It would be all right'. I thought you meant it forever... I wasn't looking for a savior, just a man whom I hoped would love me! I even wished you would leave your nice house and come and live here, instead of this 'pop-in dalliance'!"

"Oh, Tanja, I wanted only to help you have a brighter future! There's no room for a woman in my life at the moment! It's too dangerous! My assignment tonight carries a lot of risk. I repeat, I do not want to endanger you, or Kimmi!"

"Kimmi adores you! She looks up to you as the father figure she's never known!"

Karl's vivid bright eyes took on a hunted look. "Don't use emotional blackmail, please! I see it's my fault I let our relationship explode like this...you seem to expect so much from me now. It's why I keep returning, to check you're both okay. I didn't realize it's left you feeling bad. Please forgive me. I understand your need, and I'm flattered! Look, Tanja, I'll always be here for you, but not in the way you want!"

"I can't accept that! You must stay with me!" He had never heard her sound so demanding and urgent before. "Am I such a displeasing, ugly, cowed hag, that you can't love me? You men are all the same! What do I do to win your favor – beg? You're all so cock-sure of yourselves, AND I'M SICK OF IT!"

On a red-hot impulse, she moved towards a kitchen drawer and removed something that glinted sharply.

Karl didn't notice her quick action. He began: "I've tried gently, to tell you my reasons, but you won't listen – no, Tanja, STOP! Don't get so excited! Put that knife down!"

"Mummy, why is uncle Karl shouting at you?" They

hadn't heard her enter; little Kimmi stood in pink, girlie pajamas in the kitchen doorway, yawning sleepily.

Moving swiftly, Karl deliberately blocked the child's view of her mother wielding a sharp kitchen knife over him.

"Uh, Kimmi! Go back to your room, lovely – mummy will see you in a minute!"

Kimmi obeyed him docilely, without another word. She was such a sweet little thing, and nearly always did as he asked her, through their growing bond and mutual trust of one another.

He turned back to confront a rigid, scowling Tanja. Tears of frustration were gathering in her eyes.

"Look – see – she does everything for you! How can I make you care for me?"

Karl looked deflated at her obvious anguish, not able to find any soothing words that would help this rift between them. He was usually spot-on with commiserations, but Tanja's distress had swamped his mind.

Out of hopeless indignation, she cried out determinedly: "I-like-you-a-lot, Karl! I-can't-let-you-go! And I don't want to use this!"

"I won't let you use it! Calm Down! Look, don't get so distressed! I'll return when I can, and we'll talk? Yeah?"

Her stance, her dark eyes and wild dark hair seemed to flash a resistant 'no' at him.

He tried again. "Tanja, I'm an orphan, too, like you! I grew up in a children's home, here, in England. I know what it's like! As for that Croatian woman's refuge for unmarried mothers I stole you and Kimmi away from, it stank of hopelessness and despair, and I genuinely wanted to help you both! You moved me to give you a freer life! I know I haven't seen you as often as you'd like, or shown you the capital's sights, and have canceled numerous meetings because my job got in the way! I understand your need and resentment when I don't show up, or let you down. But you don't own me, not like you want to! Please realize that! Why the hell have you bottled this up for so long?"

"Because something happened today that made me think about my situation here, if you must know!"

"What situation? I thought you were settled?"

"It's been okay, for a while, I – yeah..., I'm confused over my feelings... I don't want to talk about it yet! I'm testing you!"

"Testing me! Why? I thought I'd been supportive and fair! Is it me that's confused you?"

"No, someone else. But your casual, drop-in-and-be-damned attitude towards me hasn't helped!"

"So it's my fault? We seem to be going round in circles! I haven't got time for this – I only popped in for a quick visit to see you before I went off to work! I didn't think you'd mind my coming and going like this! You haven't mentioned it before!"

Tanja sneered. "Yeah, sure! You think to walk away with no hard feelings? Don't soft-talk me! I'm capable of using this when I can't get my own way! That's how I fought back in the old days, at the children's home! We were all savages there! Your cozy explanations cuts no ice! You obviously don't want me! OKAY, Mister smart-man, I've decided...! Me and Kimmi can do without your feigned kindness and moral support! I'm finished with you! Get out, or I swear I'll will use this knife on you!"

"With Kimmi in the flat? Do you really want her to witness an act of violence towards me?"

"You know I wouldn't do that! I love her too much! But you are a disappointing prick! I hate men letting me down, and won't stand it any more! You're too smooth and shallow for me!"

"Tanja – how can you say that? I'm stung by your remark; I've done as much as I could to help you!"

She ignored him and ranted on: "To think I nearly fell for your charms! I shan't be satisfied until you leave – just go away!"

"Look – I didn't mean to upset you so much. I'll go – if that's what you obviously want! But I'm reluctant to leave you like this!"

"I'm tough! I'll get over you!"

"I like to stay in touch with Kimmi, despite this row?"

"Not a chance! Do you know I would have done anything for you! I hate being turned down! This is really the end, Karl!"

"You're not the women I thought I first knew."

"I'm myself again. The real me was hiding somewhere!"

Karl said, despairingly. "Please don't try to fight me. I understand now... We've both learned about ourselves this evening: you've lived a lie about your expectations of me, whilst I've fooled about thinking I'd found a 'domestic haven' for both of us to laugh, and share our mutual experiences with, staying as good pals together! I should have realized, been more aware, and not such a big-headed, bull-at-the-gate-type... You are a very attractive woman, and I've been a naive, narrow-minded fool, blind to your advances, hurting you in the process, thinking I was helping you and Kimmi! I was drawn to your hopeless plight by my own past experiences, liking your brave spirit, and got you this place hoping for friendship. But not love, not yet... You came along... You begged me to get you out of Croatia. I'm sorry you see it differently –"

Karl's mobile rang. He scooped it out of his jean's pocket. "Yes?"

He listened impatiently, eyeing Tanja with concerned eyes. She heard him say angrily: "You've called too early! Yes, yes, I know the place; I'm on my way now!"

He turned to Tanja with a shrug: "That's it – It's time to go! Can we make it up?"

She stared at him defiantly, but had put the knife down. "No!"

He took a deep breath, said sincerely, "Then I will miss you both – give my fondest love to Kimmi!

Please explain to her gently why I've left!"

He turned abruptly and marched from the kitchen, with a sad, disappointed sloop to his broad shoulders, her

14

vengeful cry of "Get out and don't come back!" ringing in his ears.

When the apartment door had shut behind him, she went and found Kimmi peacefully asleep, and tucked her in gently, mentally drained by her angry, stubborn tirade, wishing she'd kept her mouth shut, and her ready temper short. Had she really threatened Karl with a knife?

She'd certainly surprised him! But it was too late sighing, she was already beginning to realize she'd lost a good, loyal friend.

Maybe now was time to make up her mind; she needn't be alone for long, because of Kostas!

She pondered the coffee-shop owner's sudden asking for her hand in marriage, made to her today. Because of her desire to have a decent home for Kimmi, and gaining a bigger flat, she thought she might accept Kostas's genuine offer. He was a sincere cheerful Italian, who treated her thoughtfully and respectfully. She was ready for love, marriage, and whatever else...

She shook her head wistfully, she'd give Kostas an answer soon, and to hell with her idolized crush on Karl! She realized she'd seen Karl wearing rose-rimmed glasses, as her romantic rescuer. Hah! Karl had been right: she had fooled herself over him! He was a man who worked alone, and it was wiser for her to remember that!

# LONDON. AFTER MIDNIGHT, BAD NEWS

It was now past midnight and Karl Silverman was on his mobile, grimly aware he needed to make many calls. Resolutely, he rang a residence in the up-market area of London. When it was answered he spoke urgently: "Is that the home of Mr. Paul Wright?"

"Yes, speaking... Who's ringing at this ungodly hour?" The speaker's voice was sharp and snappy.

"It's Silverman calling, I regret to say your daughter's been kidnapped!"

There came a strangled gasp from Paul Wright, followed by a string of strong expletives. Karl listened to the older man's shock and anguish, then said: "There must be no police involved."

"What do you mean – no police?" Paul Wrights voice sounded tense and worried on the phone.

"Because I can handle this."

"You'd better be able to, Silverman. I hold you responsible for this distress!"

"I watched her – as you asked me to!"

"Then why didn't you intervene and save her?"

"I wasn't able to. The youngsters in the gang took off too quick! I think your daughter was drugged!"

"She was drugged? Hell, Leigh doesn't do drugs!"

"Her drink was probably spiked."

"I can't understand it! What do these low-life's want with her?"

"They'll want money."

"They sound too young to have organized a second kidnap!"

"It's been well-planned and executed so far. As you say, they're only the low-life's. Someone else will pay them. I believe this to be part of a bigger operation!"

"Oh, shit, my little girl, get her back before my ex learns what's happening! She'll be on my bloody back for sure!"

Karl smiled grimly to himself. "As said: they'll want money."

"Ever since that last time someone tried to take Leigh, which I told you about when I hired you, I've had some money transferred from my private bank account. It's here with me, in a safe place."

"Does your account allow a large withdrawal, or is it limited?"

"Look, it's my bank! I can reasonably do what I like with my capital. My God, Leigh's worth it! I love that girl! I need her back in London, safe and sound, man!"

"I'll call you when I have more news."

"Do that! I'll be up most of the bloody night, worrying. Just make sure my baby's safe! Get her for me!"

"There's another innocent girl involved as well."

"Another girl? Never mind her! Just get my girl home safely, man! I don't care about the other one!"

"But I do!" Karl replied feelingly. He snapped off his mobile, fuming. These millionaires! Only their tight, smug little world mattered to them!

Thoughtfully, he called two more people. One was to a London number, the other was abroad.

# WEST SUSSEX. DUMPED IN A CELLAR!

"Ar-oh! My head!" Leigh moaned, coming to.

Fran was instantly beside her, on the cold stone-paved floor, where Leigh had been unceremoniously dumped, her hands untied now, asking anxiously: "Oh, Leigh! Thank God you're awake! Are you okay?"

"I could spew up! Ugh! Where am I – it's so cold here! What the hell has happened to me?"

"I don't know. A boy and two girls stuck us in a black car and drove off with us!"

"I kinda remember... They gave me a drink? Tequila?"

"Did you drink it all?"

"Only some. I felt funny right away."

"They must have put something in it. When you were dumped in the car, you slept like a baby. I wish I could have done!"

"You stayed awake?" Leigh's blue eyes widened. "Did you see where we are?"

"We're in some dark old cellar, I think."

"No, I mean, did you see any road signs?"

"I saw a white sign that read 'West Sussex' in the car's headlights. We turned down a rough track shortly after. They told me to go down some stairs, and the girls carried you down, awkwardly and dumped you with me."

"Couldn't you have escaped?"

"It would have been bloody awkward – I was held at knife-point!"

"Oh, sod! This is horrible!"

They were silent, shivering in their thin party frocks, both assuming they were being held below ground somewhere. Neither heard the wind pick up outside.

Fran said: "I can't think why this has happened!"

Leigh rubbed her aching head. "I can!"

"How do you mean?"

"My daddy's rich, very rich!"

"Oh? Like, millionaire rich?"

"Yeah! You've heard of the Silverdale Society?"

"I've an account with them! You mean your dad works for Silverdale?"

"He owns it! He's gotta whole chain of banks!"

Fran hastily put two and two together. In a small voice she said: "Oh no! We've been kidnapped!"

"I've been kidnapped, you mean? Someone's tried to do it before, too!"

"Yeah? What happened?"

"Our chauffeur saved me, and the man who attacked him ran away."

"Hell!"

"I can't think how you got roped into this? There's no one to save me this time! I'm sunk!"

"Me, and the man who was dancing with us followed you outside. I interfered with the gang's getaway, shouting at them! Because of that, they took me, too!"

"Wow! You were brave! Did our dancing man try to stop them?"

"He was too shocked! I saw him contacting someone on his mobile as we sped off!"

"Might be hope for us? God, the last kidnap attempt was awful! Now it's happened again I could scream!"

"So could I, but I don't think anyone would hear us down here! What are we going to do?"

"Shush!"

Both girls stiffened fearfully. A key was being turned in the lock...

# WEST SUSSEX. TAKEN AWAY

The fire place in the shadowy ruined cottage living room glowed a dusky red in the candlelight. The girl with plaits the boy had called 'Sal', and the moody-looking dark girl he'd labeled 'Jaz', were listlessly scrolling on their mobiles sitting at a rickety table, near the small fire the boy had kindled in the grate.

Despite the faint heat of the fire the room smelt of damp and mold. It was colder inside the cottage than out in the balmy air, and everyone was chilled stiff and bored, waiting impatiently for their tedious assignment to end, and to claim their illicit payment!

The boy wearing glasses, was at the window peering out at the now gloomy, wind-ridden landscape, where silhouetted trees waved and whispered in the breeze, and strange animal noises could be heard from the open countryside, despite the sullen airless wind.

A light colored people carrier had drawn up. It flashed its headlights on and off twice.

"They're here." There was a note of relief in the boy's voice. The two girls watched silently, as he confidently slid the bolt on the old wooden front door and let in two men of Arabian description. The Arabs were brown-skinned, swarthy looking with short dark beards. They explored the room's gloomy surroundings with sharp, flashing eyes before they relaxed their alert guard.

One of the Arabs spoke in English: "You shouldn't have lit a fire. It draws attention."

"It was only to keep us warm. It's cold in here!"

"Cold!" There was scorn in the foreigner's voice. "It's warm! No more excuses! Where is the girl? We only need one; now we've heard you've acquired two? Why?"

The boy looked sulky. "We had no choice, the second silly bitch got in the way! What will you do with her?"

The first man shrugged. "Lock her in and leave her here!"

At his uncaring suggestion the two girls glanced apprehensively at each other. Sal murmured: "We're miles from anywhere! She could die here! I don't want to be involved with murder!"

The first man shrugged again, looking bored. "So what's new? If she's a true virgin we could take her with us and sell her to sex marketers!"

Sal shuddered. "That sounds even worse! Brian, you didn't tell me it would be like this?"

Brian looked uncomfortable.

The second man demanded: "Lead us to the girls! It wasn't planned, but we'll take the other one with us. She may be useful!"

"This way." Brian was eager for the men to leave with their burdens.

The moody girl, Jaz, suddenly stood up, announcing imperiously: "I want my money! Where is it?"

The girl with plaits followed suit. "Yeah! You owe us now! We've done the job!"

Without warning, the second man drew something shiny from his trouser belt. Without compunction he coolly and coldly shot down the moody girl and the girl with plaits. The shocked boy saw a surprised look appear on their young teenage faces as they both crumpled to the floor, almost in a kind of slow motion, without making a sound, leaving their switched-on mobiles glowing on the table.

"That is your payment." The second man said succinctly. He swung his gun onto the startled boy, who, fearing the worst, began to back slowly away, his hands shielding his horrified face.

The Arab ordered, curtly: "Take us to the girls!"

Trembling with fear, Brian did so, expecting any minute to be shot too.

Now aware of his danger, Brian fumbled at the cellar door. It opened creakily, revealing two frightened, startled girls clutching each other.

The first man swung a torch over them. The girls blinked, not seeing a thing beyond the dazzling beam. They hadn't heard the gun go off upstairs as the walls of this old cottage were of thick stone.

"You two! Out! Out, quickly!"

The second Arab asked his companion: "What about the boy?"

"Get the girls tied up, and I'll sort the boy out!"

As the girls timidly filed out from their cold prison, terrified, seeing the men's guns trained on them, the first Arab ushered Brian at gunpoint into the cellar.

"Y-your not leaving me down here, are you?"

"That is right!"

"Please – no – I beg you! Don't leave –"

But the Arab slammed the door shut. Unconcerned, he locked it and threw away the key, which landed in a dark dusty corner of the passage.

Not comprehending what had happened upstairs, the girls trembled as they found their hands tied behind them for a second time that night.

They could hear the boy banging on the door but were powerless to help him, or themselves.

"What is happening?" Leigh mumbled, shaking with fear.

"You are both going to sleep for a while." The Arab with the gun replied matter-of-factly, as if tying up women in dark cellar corridors was an every day occurrence.

Leigh shrunk away from him, as he inspected the injection he held in his hand with his torch. Her eyes widened in shocked horror when she saw it.

"You're not injecting me with that thing, are you? I won't have it – HELP! HELP!"

"Yell all you like, no one will hear you!" He advanced towards her.

For the girls, this chilling scene was like a nightmare from hell. Fran sobbed, trying to wrest her tied wrists undone, which was hopeless. The second man held on to her tightly. "You're next, you might as well stop struggling!"

Leigh was still calling for help. Suddenly, she yelped as the needle found it's target. Within seconds she was slumped against the passageway's grainy stone walls, comatose.

Oh God, it was her turn! Fran could do nothing to help herself, as she felt the needle enter her vein. Soon, she was as out and out as Leigh was, leaning hopelessly against the old cottage's damp wall, in danger of sliding down it, but held up by one of the men.

"A good night's work!" The second Arab said, complacently.

The two men picked the girls up, and carried them towards their waiting vehicle, passing the group's grubby Mazda, and leaving the boy to shout himself hoarse in the cellar, thudding as hard as he could against the heavy wooden door.

The men could hear his banging as they left. Unperturbed, they placed their helpless prisoners in the back of the people carrier, and strapped them in securely, so they wouldn't roll around too much. The girls didn't feel a thing – they were dead to the world.

The Arab men drove them to a disused air-strip not far from the run-down cottage, both congratulating themselves on a mission well accomplished.

# WEST SUSSEX. INFORMATION

Having his own ways and means, Karl Silverman had managed to follow the girls trail to West Sussex. On his speedy journey, he'd passed a pair of high, rusty, dilapidated, buckled iron gates, hanging off their concrete posts, beyond which lay a disused airfield, left desecrated and abandoned in this part of the countryside.

It looked the perfect place to attract a lover's rendezvous, tramps, gypsies – and kidnappers.

It came to mind the first kidnap attempt had used a plane of some kind...

This empty airfield he noted, was very near to a derelict cottage that his electronic strategic information dictated the girls might have been taken to. He could dimly see the ramshackle cottage's forlorn, lonely shape picked out by his car's bright headlights, as he stopped outside its knee-high tangled garden and overgrown shrubbery.

Stealthily investigating outside, Karl came to the conclusion this run-down property appeared to be empty.

He could smell the blood as he quietly entered the old crumbling building, torch in hand, noting it's warped, splintered wooden door had been left ajar, as if people had left hurriedly, with an intent purpose.

The fire gave off a wispy smoke. He felt the grate, still warm. Then his senses sharpened to high alert as he heard the thudding below his feet.

It was action time, and he quickly reacted to it!

He had thrust Tanja's sharp words from his mind hours ago, and was acting with pure professional purpose now.

He could see from his torch that there was nothing he could do for the dead girls, lying haphazardly where they had been shot, on the grubby, foot-scarred, ripped lino floor.

Participants or innocents, death had visited them without warning, abruptly cutting off their dreams and plans he noted grimly. Rage was building in his chest.

He lifted his own personal Ruger LCP, ready for trouble. Most times he worked alone, and tonight was no exception, apart from letting 'the den' guys and CIUSO know where he was, and liaising with others overseas, but the crass, senseless murder of the two girls got to him, and it was in this mood that he found and descended the cellar steps, ready for any danger.

The stone steps ended in a narrow passageway. Karl shone the torch at the cellar door.

Immediately, a male youth's worried voice cried out: "Who's that? Christ, let me out – I'm suffocating!"

"Not yet; I've questions to ask. Where are the two girls you kidnapped from the disco?"

"Uh – what two girls?"

"Well, certainly not the two who've been shot to death upstairs! I'm after the young women I saw you bundle into your car outside the night club!"

"Bloody hell, that's was miles away! Back in London! How could you follow us here?"

"I don't tell scum like you my ways and means! Where are the girls, or you're in deep trouble with me! I'll leave you here, as the real kidnappers intended! You don't want to die, too, do you? No water, no food, no toilet!"

"Oh, God! I thought you'd come to rescue me? Please get me out!" There was panic in Brian's voice.

"If you don't tell me who's set this up, I'll go – you'll never see me again!"

Karl deliberately shuffled his feet. The boy heard his movements and cried out: "Wait! I-I'll tell you what I know! But let me out! I'm getting claustrophobic!"

"You've got five seconds!"

"Aw, c'mon – let me out first?"

"No, not if you still have that knife on you!"

"Shit, all right!" The boy sulkily told Karl what he

knew. It had been arranged by someone Brian didn't know, for foreign men to arrive at this rendezvous tonight, and take the girls away. He wasn't sure where.

It wasn't much. Karl's torch found the key and he unlocked the door, dissatisfied with the lack of information.

The boy hadn't mentioned the airstrip, and Karl assumed the girls kidnappers had used it to make their getaway – if the last kidnap was anything to go by. These men could have abandoned their car nearby somewhere, which he didn't have time to look for. He'd have to ask CIUSO to investigate for him. The two girls could be anywhere by now! He was worried about that.

Brian came out cautiously when he saw Silverman's gun in the torchlight. Karl frisked him expertly, quickly finding the knife, which he placed further back along the dark, dusty passageway for CIUSO men to find when they arrived here. He'd have to call them and tell them this location.

Karl asked the distraught teenager: "What type of car did they have?"

"Christ, man! it was dark outside! Some kind of people-carrier, I think. It was long and big."

"Where will the girls be taken to if these foreign men used the airstrip nearby?"

"What airstrip? Jesus – I don't know!"

"What nationality were the foreigners?"

"Arabs! They wore suits, and spoke to us in English, and they had bloody guns! The sod shot Sal and Jazz without warning and locked me in here! They didn't fucking care about us at all, and wouldn't hand over the money that Jazz asked for!"

"Ah!" Karl managed a grim shrug. Things were looking up! Having Arab's on the scene confirmed something he already knew! Now he had a better idea...

He said, deliberately: "When you wake up, you'll find a special police unit here. They'll remove the girls bodies, and find the knife with your fingerprints on it! You're guilty as hell! You'll be charged for your part in this kidnapping!"

"Christ! It was only for the money! What d'yuh mean – when I wake up?"

Karl didn't hesitate, he punched the boy swiftly on his jaw. He didn't like to see young females shot for no reason. "Let that be a lesson to you," he said, as Brian was felled by the blow. "Don't meddle in things you can't control!"

He left the teenager lying concussed in the drafty passageway, as he thumbed his mobile, ringing the urgent numbers he needed...

# LONDON, SATURDAY. SURPRISE CALL

"I don't give a shit if it's 4am in London – it's 8am out here, and I want to speak to my daughter, you ass-hole!"

Expecting to hear from the kidnappers, Paul Wright had quickly grabbed his kitchen phone, but was disappointed when he heard his ex-wife's strident voice. He was used to her coarse opening gambits over the wire and he flashed back instantly: "Don't call me names, you bitch! You can't! I mean – she's fast asleep, Serena. I can't wake her up at this time of the morning!"

"Oh, don't be such a boring worm, Paul! You've let me speak to her before when I've called early!"

"She er, only went to bed a couple of hours ago..."

"So? She's young, she'll get over it! Night club was it? Its a pity she can't drive yet! She'll be wanting her own pad soon!"

"Over my dead body! I don't like to let her out of my sight, after you-know what happened!"

"That was a few weeks back. It can't happen again! You're paranoid, Paul!"

"Am I? Don't bet on it – things could be happening right now!" Paul hinted, darkly.

"What are you expecting, you melancholy man – another ambush? And why are you up in the early hours?"

She'd caught him unawares. "Er... I couldn't sleep! You know; business, business."

"Funny time for it! Don't your bank's ever shut? Your sighing again, are you sure you're all right? Nothings wrong with Leigh, is there? Because if there's any boy trouble I'll fly over and sort it out!"

"I know you will! You've made that plain before! But I must keep the line free, in case..."

"Why? In case of – what? This business of yours doesn't involve Leigh, does it?"

Paul sighed gustily again. Serena had an uncanny way of ferreting the truth from him. Now, she'd keep on at him all the time unless he offered her a satisfying explanation!

But he'd hesitated too long, and sensing something wrong, she was now on the warpath.

"Let me speak to Leigh, Paul. I'll keep it short." Her voice had sharpened.

He said, heavily: "You can't. I lied – she isn't here."

"What's going on, Paul? What do you mean she isn't there?"

Serena heard his anguish then: "I didn't want to tell you, Serena. She's been bloody kidnapped again – spirited away! I'm beside myself, so help me! Leigh's been taken!"

# ABU DHABI, SATURDAY.
# WAITING EXPECTANTLY

Serena Wright replaced the ornate gold receiver on its old-fashioned prongs, with a secret smile playing around her red lipstick-stained mouth.

She said to the dark-haired, slightly plump Arab male sitting on the plush white curbed sofa beside her: "Our house-guest is due soon, my love! Your men have done it this time! They've actually managed to kidnap my daughter, and another girl, apparently!"

Serena's plump handsome partner frowned slightly. "Another girl taken as well? What are Emir and Ameen playing at? Is this other female after a free ride? Let's hope her parents have plenty of money, eh? Maybe I'll use her in my schemes! Ah, well, sweet-ling, it doesn't matter, we shall be very rich soon! A pity the first plan failed... But we're moving at last! We can feast like Midas – on plenty of gold!"

He looked younger, more robust than the carefully made-up Serena, and smiled in a cunning way as he picked up two fluted, amber-shaded glasses that held pink gin. "This is so good! Here's to us my little Haiwa! You have played your part well! I am pleased with you!"

Serena patted her damp, dyed golden curls, wondering if the air conditioning was working properly. It was so hot already! "I always wanted to be an actress!" She twanged, imitating an American voice.

But then she was serious. "When are you going to ask for the kidnap money for Leigh, Asad?"

"When I receive my bundle and see the merchandise, not a minute before!"

"Hang on, Leigh isn't some wrapped-up package that you can untie at your leisure and gloat over! Assure me, lover; Leigh will be okay? Your men won't harm her?"

"She'll be okay, little Haiwa. Ask yourself – have I ever let you down?"

"Yes, sometimes!"

Asad laughed. "Ah, so truthful you are! But you always forgive me!"

She laughed with him easily. "That's because I like wicked men!"

"Wicked rich men!" He corrected dryly, downing his celebratory breakfast drink in three quick swallows. "I must go out now, sweet-ling! I'll meet you here, late morning! Arrive about noon, and I'll bring back some champagne, for us to properly toast our venture together!"

"Late morning! But can't I come in the cool of the evening when everyone else is at large, enjoying their day!"

"No. I shall be busy then. Stay cool. I'll turn up the air conditioning just for you, and we'll have our very own private party for two!"

"But, Asad –"

"Don't pester me sweet-ling. Remember, I'm doing all this for you! I'll make it as passionate and romantic as I can!"

"Oh, yeah. That's what I like about you, Asad – such a playboy! I can't wait! You know how much I like being with you!"

Asad returned later that morning, pleased with his clandestine arrangements, and met a wilting Serena waiting for him outside his penthouse. After a rich lunch shared with her, plus several glasses of foamy champagne, they huddled and cuddled 'with passion', as Asad had promised. Then his phone rang. Relaxed and amiable, he picked up his gold receiver calmly, smiling at Serena, who was again beside him on his comfortable white lounge sofa, clinging to his free arm intimately. "Hello?"

His rugged face darkened as the voice at the other end gave him some bad news. Serena didn't hear what was said, but Asad asked curtly, in some alarm: "Are you saying that he's arrived in our country today, the man I was warned about? I see... So you followed his taxi, but lost it somewhere in the Al Maqtaa sector – you stupid fool! It's crucial that I know where this foreigner is staying, so I can thwart his plans! Find the taxi driver who picked him up and have him questioned! Get back to me as quickly as you can!"

An apologizing voice the other end told Asad something that made him sit up straighter, with brightened interest.

"He has what, a girlfriend and child, in England? That is interesting! You might be able to make 'arrangements' for them – on my behalf! Do you know where they live? Good. Have his people taken somewhere quiet, a rented cottage in the British countryside will do! Start organizing this now! Let me know what is happening. We'll have a lever on him over his woman and child! Or we can arrange a suitable 'accident' for this man if he starts poking his nose in my affairs! He's in my country now, he'll have to bend to our laws – if you get what I mean! I will have him shot!"

Serena had been listening. She watched her lover ungraciously crash the phone down on its cradle, looking rattled. She asked curiously: "Trouble, Asad?"

He shot her a disarming smile, hiding his seething temper. "Nothing for you to worry about, sweet-ling! I have everything under control! Let us finish our celebration with this fine champagne!"

Serena relaxed and beamed at him. "Yes, lets! I relish our times together, it's so hard to live apart from you! How soon can I move in permanently, my love?"

Asad carried on smiling into Serena's heavily made-up eyes. "Very soon, sweet-ling, very soon! If we uphold government laws correctly you can legally take my name!"

"Sod your laws! They're bloody frustrating! You and I know you're not as above-board as you make out! You can't tell me all your people are puritans here? Bet loads of them co-habit and share their bedrooms and ignore Islamic law, in this day and age!"

Asad shrugged lightly, looking bored. He inspected his glossy nails before replying. "Be patient, Serena! I do have my reputation to consider! Things will get even better for us soon, when my plan begins to unfold. We'll have so much more to spend!"

Serena beamed again, snuggling closer to him. "You're right. I'm looking forward to that! I mustn't be petty about your country's old-fashioned attitudes, today! Cheers, Asad!"

# FLYING FAR AWAY. PRISONERS!

Leigh awoke to an extremely dry mouth and a jaw-splitting headache. She found she was strapped in on some kind of narrow bunk-bed. Around her, engines hummed in a quietly inoffensive way.

She squinted over and saw Fran, also strapped in, apparently fast asleep, her untidy blond tresses pillowing her head. She looked comfortable and relaxed, which annoyed Leigh, who yelled: "Fran! Fran! Wake up, for Christ sake!"

"Uh! W-what –?"

"Fran!"

"Oh! Jesus – my head! Where are we?"

In answer to Fran's question a curtain that had been covering a small opening was scraped aside.

A swarthy bearded face peered at them, then withdrew for a moment.

Leigh was about to speak, when the Arab returned, carrying a loaded tray.

"My goodness!" Leigh spoke her thoughts out loud, sarcastically, before she realized she was addressing one of their kidnappers: "He must be civilized – he's bringing us some coffee, I hope!"

It was coffee, with cream too, and what looked like buttered croissants. The Arab put the tray down on a small alcove bench between the bunk-beds and proceeded to unlatch both girls straps.

Disorientated, they unsteadily sat upright, moaning at their headaches. The man left them to their warm breakfast. The girls fell on the food without further ado, grateful for the hot strong black coffee. As they finished eating they hit some kind of turbulence. Leigh's eyes widened. "I think we're on a plane? How weird is that?"

"Like – weird! I thought the same, but where on earth are we going?" Fran looked scared. She was out of her depth and knew it. Leigh was the same. Both girls couldn't get their heads around what had happened to them.

Practically, Fran said: "Least it's warmer here! I was so cold in that cellar!"

"Me, too. I can't remember ever being so cold as last night – was it only last night?"

"Yes, it was last night. God knows the time now – my phone's been taken, so I can't tell. Oh, Leigh – where are they taking us? Why did I get involved in this?" Fran's mouth wobbled.

Leigh patted Fran on the arm. "I'm sorry – it's all my fault! I should have known better than go to 'Minks' on my own!"

"I just wish I wasn't here, that's all! It's a nightmare come true! Oh! What's that?"

The Arab had returned again and both girls knew a frisson of fear.

Leigh said suddenly: "The tray – we'll bash him on the head with it and escape!"

"We can't." Fran was more practical. "Even if we did that, we still can't get off this plane!"

Leigh's shoulders dropped. "You're right. I wasn't thinking!"

Two Arab men had now squeezed together into the girls sleeping apartment-cum-cubbyhole, one of whom the girls recognized as bringing them their food and drink. Both men had discarded their suit jackets in favor of short-sleeved shirts. In a kind of dumb horror the girls found themselves staring down the chunky barrel of one of their flashy automatic hand-guns...

# ABU DHABI, SATURDAY. ARRANGEMENTS

Karl Silverman walked via the retail corridor in Abu Dhabi International Airport, exiting the terminal building carrying only his light-weight nylon Nike gym bag on his broad back.

He was remembering that Abu Dhabi was the most expensive place to live in the Middle East, with Dubai coming a close second. The cost of living in Abu Dhabi was high. This City was part of the United Arab Emirates. It was one of the Persian Gulf states, a desert country in the south east of the Arabian Peninsula with a coastline at the Persian Gulf (Arab Gulf) and the Gulf of Oman. The UAE borders Oman and Saudi Arabia, and has maritime borders with Iran.

His bag had been searched at the airport. He knew that items such as narcotics, poppy seeds, cocaine, hashish, heroin and hallucination pills were banned in the UAE. Also, such foods as pork, and any goods from boycotted countries brought with intention to sell; Israeli goods, logos and trademarks, crude ivory and rhinoceros horn. All fruits, vegetables, plants and plant materials had to be declared when approaching Customs.

It had been a mad scramble to get here. His people working at CIUSO had booked him on a very early morning flight, and issued him with certain passes, visa's, cards and a satellite phone license for use in the UAE. He'd gone home to change and pick up his passport, and had managed to eat a quick sandwich.

Luckily, he had had a combined vaccine for diphtheria, tetanus, pertussis, measles, mumps, rubella and polio, also the vaccine for Hepatitis A, B, and rabies, some months back. He'd been fit to go.

It was very hot. He was nearly in the same clothes he'd worn to the night club the evening before.

At home he'd quickly shrugged into a light blue open-necked polo top, and now wore bootleg jeans. All his personal luggage, including specially-designed items produced by 'the den' were in his gym bag. He'd thrown in a pair of knee-length Bermuda shorts as an afterthought, and picked up a navy blue cap for his shaved head.

Arabs take pride in maintaining their historical dress code and it was an offense in the UAE if you wore skin-tight jeans, slashed knee jeans, or any item of clothing or skirt above the knee in public places.

He suspected the Government here held their own surveillance practices, blocking some social media platforms, and social networking services and dating sites too.

The only new object he'd brought at the airport were some Jack Browne sunglasses costing around 254Dirhams. He would have to declare all goods bought here on his return home – whenever that would be!

Part of his plan was to get a gun when he reached Abu Dhabi. Technically, he wasn't a police Operative here; he had no powers – except with those authorities he was liaising with on his mobile. It was illegal in the UAE to carry firearms in a public place, even if it was licensed, and if a gun was found on him, he'd be imprisoned for at least half a year, and would have to pay a fine of around 15,000Dirhams.

He'd called from the airport, a certain number on his mobile, and ascertained from a middle eastern ex-pat agent involved with CIUSO, who lived close to the airport, that he could call and pick up a lightweight gun from him, plus a cleverly forged license made out in his name, mainly because he knew he'd need one. He was up against killers.

He'd had so much on his mind and so much to do he hadn't expected to be followed from the airport...

Ignoring his Arab-dressed follower, who didn't seem a very good tracker, Karl strode across the pedestrian corridor and into The Premier Inn, where he found a member of staff who could assist him.

"I'm looking for Rachid Al Alamin. I think he works here?"

"Ah no, sir. Rachid left about a week ago."

"I see, do you know where I can find him?"

"Yes, sir. Probably in the bar of The Force's Hotel, drowning his sorrows! I think he was sacked!"

"Why?"

"He was unreliable in his work!"

Karl shook his head ruefully. "That sounds like Rachid! Thank you." He gave the helpful young Arab waiter a good handful of smaller loose Dirhams taken from his pocket. He secretly picked up his gun from the agent near the airport, then walked outside to find a waiting taxi.

He hailed one that had the old taxi colors painted on its roof, and ordered the elderly driver to take him to The Force's Hotel. Instead of only ten minutes, it took about twenty minutes more to reach his destination, as the Arab driver had gone a round-about way to the hotel on Karl's order's. They avoided the Al Maqtaa area. This meant they lost the car trailing Karl. Pleased with the driver's discretion, Karl gave him a fifteen per-cent tip, although he didn't have to. It was gratefully appreciated.

He made straight for the bar, which was cool and shaded with the air conditioning on a high setting, and walked straight past a white-haired man sitting in a comfortable lounge chair, who looked surprised to see him.

World War 11 RAF veteran, Derrick 'Dickie' Fairs, sat relaxing in the cool bar of the Force's Hotel. He had his reading glasses on, and he was wearing his navy-colored cardigan against the coolness of the air-conditioning. It was very hot outside the hotel, stifling in fact.

He was sipping his cup of tea, (for which he'd supplied the tea bag from a batch he'd brought with him), when he'd spied Karl Silverman walking casually into the bar area.

This man the ex squadron leader so keenly noticed carried, slung over his shoulder, a holdall in the shape of a large gym bag. He looked as if he was traveling light – with a purpose.

He strode solidly across to a grizzled Arab, who sat with hunched back on a stool beside the bar, and slapped him on his shoulder.

Intrigued, Derrick thought of standing up to surprise Karl, but he was tired from the heat of the day outside, and it was certainly cooler in here! He shifted slightly, to hear what was said, as he was sitting near enough. He wasn't intending to pry, but the years he served in the RAF during the second world war, and then a job with the police in London, had taught him to be discreet as well as honest. If he knew Karl Silverman, this looked like some kind of surprise meeting!

"Hello, Rachid." Karl Silverman said, heartily.

Rachid spluttered into his iced coke, choking so harshly, he coughed badly. "Mr Karl! What are you doing here?"

"Looking for you. A job's come up."

Rachid's dark eyes narrowed nervously, as if a shutter had been pulled down.

"Er.., what kind of job? I told you, I wasn't going to do any more work for you!"

"Why not? I pay well!"

"Because I don't want to get in any trouble with the gangs and thugs you mix with!"

Karl laughed. Derrick remembered that laugh; easygoing, relaxed. "There's no 'trouble' in this job, I promise you!"

"I got a twisted elbow and a black eye the last time I worked for you!"

"Peace be on you, man, it won't happen again! Would 300Dirhams suit you?"

A greedy look came into Rachid's dark eyes. "Make it more, and I might consider."

Derrick watched Karl count out an impressive amount and placed it, rolled-up, in the other man's eager hand.

"Don't spend it all at once on private booze at home, or you'll need another license for it! I merely want you to find out something about a certain person, and then find out where this person's father is living now – I'll do the rest!"

Despite himself, Rachid looked interested. So did Derrick. "Who is this person?" Rachid asked.

Karl told him a name, and Rachid's rangy, shifty eyes opened wide in surprise.

Rachid pursed his lips. "He's a well-known wealthy man in these parts! I had no idea there was anything shady –"

Karl put a finger to his lips. "It's precisely why I need to find his father!"

"And then what?"

"I want to meet the father, and I want you to ask this father a very personal question for me!"

"Which is?"

"I'm just about to tell you!" Karl bent down and whispered something in Rachid's ear.

He asked out loud: "Are you game for the job, Rachid?"

Rachid sighed with weary resignation, shaking his shrouded head. "I'm not happy about the question you wish me to ask! How do I explain myself, to inquire about such a personal thing – politely, to an Arab of the dessert? Especially if this nomad announces his guilt to me! He will not want the authorities to know his secret, kept silent for many years! Even now, if he was found out, he could be punished severely!"

"I'm counting on your discretion, Rachid. Keep quiet what he tells you, but report back to me what he says, okay? It's important I know the true facts. My plans rest on it!"

"Yeah, okay Mr Karl!"

"Good man!"

Judging this to be his moment, Derrick rose slowly and stiffly to his feet. He called, softly: "Hey, Karl? Fancy seeing you here!"

Karl spun round and did a double-take.

"Hell, if it's not my old work-advisor, squadron leader Dickie Fairs? What a fantastic surprise to find you in this place! Have you just come in, or have you been hiding here, and heard what I've just told Rachid?

"You know me better than that, young man, to charge in, listening to your covert operations! I've other things to do!" Derrick scolded him in a friendly way. "Admittedly, I've been here since early morning, and I did overhear enough just now, to wonder what kind of mission you were on this time! It's been a few years since I last saw you!"

Karl grinned, showing excellent teeth. "Yeah, I've been busy! It's another mission! I'm after two young women who've been kidnapped and taken here! They're somewhere in Abu Dhabi."

"Really? I assume they've been taken by the man whose name you whispered to your friend here?"

"Possibly! I've yet to make sure. Are you on your own, Dickie?"

"I've been staying the week with my son and his wife. They've gone to Dubai today – whether they'll get in with a normal visa, I don't know, but I was too tired to face any more travel yet!"

Karl's calm brown eyes took in the walking stick set beside the squadron leader's table. "How are you faring?" He asked kindly. "You look well!"

"I'm recuperating at the moment. Some time back I broke my left ankle on the stairs at home, hence the walking stick!" Derrick beckoned to it casually, propped against his armchair. "I'm in my nineties now, you know!"

"Are you really? Well done, Dickie, it's great to see you again! Look, I have a half-hour to spare, can I offer you a drink for old time's sake!"

"That would be nice. Are you working alone, or in a group!"

His innocent question reminded Karl of Tanja. "I'm on

my own – for now!" He said, abruptly.

Rachid interrupted their conversation. "I suppose I'd better go and earn my keep!" He glanced shrewdly at Derrick, then Karl. "I take it you two are good friends?"

"Absolutely," answered Karl with another flash of teeth. "Believe it or not, this gentleman enlisted for World War two at the age of 17, if I remember rightly. He lied about his age when he joined up!"

Rachid shot Derrick a respectful glance and asked. "You look a man of rank! Were you a captain?"

"No. Royal Air force, Squadron leader."

"Then I salute you as a fighting man who won victory for his country!"

Derrick accepted this admiring compliment with a dignified nod of his long-haired, well-groomed white head, where a noticeable liver-spotted birth mark flamed under his right eye on his aged, pale-faced features.

"I'm proud to say that Derrick took part in the battle of Britain," Karl continued, "in the police force he monitored some of my missions from my murky past! Didn't you, Dickie?"

"That's right, Karl. Although saying you had a 'murky' past implies I did too! I beg to differ! But as your mentor in some awkward times, I would often give you good sound advice, which you never took...you always were a difficult bugger!"

Karl Silverman laughed outright. He said to Rachid: "We have some good stories to tell each other!"

"I can't hang around to hear them. I'll be leaving, Mr Karl!"

As Rachid moved away, Karl took hold of Derrick's arm, and gently re-seated him.

"I'll get you a beer." He told his friend. "To toast old times with!"

Finding himself seated again, Derrick asked: "Do you have time to reminisce?"

"For you I do, Dickie. I owe my promotion, and subsequent position in CIUSO due to your help!"

Derrick nodded sagely. "I think I'd like to hear of this, your most recent adventure? Talking about our old jobs in the past can be exhausting!"

"You want to know about this job?"

Derrick smiled gently and nodded again.

"Sure. We could do with a drink – it's so hot!" Karl peeled away part of his polo shirt from his sweaty chest to allow some coolness and went to the bar and ordered two beers. Soon, he was sitting in the next armchair opposite the man who had befriended and aided his career.

He took a long sip of his drink. "I think this might be a story of greed and, possibly, betrayal…" He began.

# THE FORCES HOTEL, ABU DHABI. STARTLING NEWS

Derrick listened attentively to Karl's story, sipping slowly at his beer, interrupting Karl from time to time. As Karl paused to take a long swig at his drink, his elderly friend spoke in awe: "Are you telling me these youngsters slipped the kidnapped girl a Mickey Finn in her drink?"

"They spiked it, yes!"

"The young devils!"

"This was a finely honed kidnap this time, using youngsters to trap youngsters! That takes a lot of planning!"

"So, in your mind, it was another 'arranged', well-organized kidnap?"

"Yeah!"

"It's an interesting tale. You're in at the deep end again, chasing crooks to your heart's content, eh, Karl? Did you enjoy your energetic dancing with the girls? You were always a keep-fit fanatic!"

"Let's just say the evening was great, but what happened afterwards wasn't so good!"

"Go on – tell me!"

Karl did, and Derrick tutted in disbelief. "The sheer audacity of those youngsters, taking both girls like that! You say you couldn't help them in any way?"

"No, I screwed up there. Having one taken is bad enough, but two!"

"They didn't need two girls! Why did they take the second one?"

"She tried to be a hero. She got in the way."

"What a blasted shame! She should have stopped to

think what she was doing, and save herself from this upset. Youngsters are always in a hurry these days! What are you going to do about her?"

Karl sighed. "She's caused me some grief, I admit... I can't let on too much, but I've a few tricks up my sleeve, which might help her, and the other one!"

"Awkward to try and rescue two girls! Do go on, Karl!"

A few sentences later, Derrick mused: "It sounds like the rich girls father has staked all his money to get her back safely. Why take the girls to West Sussex? What's there?"

"There's a disused airfield in that area, ideal for a light machine to land in darkness, unseen. It's too much of a coincidence that the old tumbledown cottage was nearby. As I explained to you earlier, a plane of some sort was used in the first attempted kidnap."

"Yes, I see. You think they were carried off in a small jet?"

"A private one, yes!"

"Well, someone's gone to an awful lot of trouble to grab them! It's astonishing!"

Derrick noisily sucked in his cheeks when Karl reluctantly mentioned the teenage girls shot in cold blood at the derelict cottage.

"That's shocking, Karl, this stinks of professional racketeers! I can see now – somebody high up, with plenty of money has masterminded this caper! Now you have my total interest!"

Karl nodded, he quaffed his ice-cold beer and carried on. Derrick listened hard to what followed, announcing, when Karl paused again. "Yes, I fear I would have knocked this boy out, too – if it had been war-time! I can't get over these murderous swine's, to shoot young women like that! What a diabolical thing to do! What kind of crass, uncaring thugs are they?"

"Seasoned killers, gun-trained psychopaths? Take your pick! I know what I'm up against now. I was angry at myself for not being there earlier to prevent those kids deaths! It's such a waste of life!"

"Now, now, Karl, you can't blame yourself! I'm sure you did all you could!"

"I tried. Despite being trained to kill, I see all life as valuable and precious. As a special operator trying to work within the line of duty, it's hard to balance your own instincts when faced with murderous situations made by ignorant clowns who use weapons of terror, to control and kill others without a conscious thought! It creates power. For these type of thugs, it's all too easy to use a knife, or a gun, when they've got their fingers on the trigger!"

"I know, life and death have to be confronted in your job." Derrick muttered. "The difference with you is that you stay on the right side! Don't forget that, Karl – you're a good man!"

Karl sighed. "I felt like using that stupid teenager as a punch-bag last night, because of those dead girls... Luckily, I held my temper and only knocked him out!"

"I realize that. I'm pleased of the man you've become! Some operatives get frustrated, hard-boiled and heavy-handed when carrying out orders, but you're more caring and mature than them!"

Karl flashed Derrick a grateful grin. "I'm glad to see you again, Dickie! You always say the right things!"

Derrick nodded, smiling, as Karl's mobile rang. He picked it up from the table immediately.

Watching Karl's handsome, tanned face, Derrick became alerted by his friend's sudden agitated manner, and he noticed in dismay, that a deep shock reflected in Karl's wide brown eyes. His body, normally at ease and casual, had become tense with sudden distress as he straightened to listen intently to his message.

He demanded sharply: "Fuck – when did this happen?"

His voice was nerve-sharp, making Derrick wonder what was up...

# ABU DHABI, SATURDAY.
# MENACING QUESTIONS

Karl's taxi driver had been an older-generation Arab, who lived on his own in a suburban district in Al Falah City.

He was taking time off from his rounds, enjoying his lunch outside his home under a ragged awning, when three Arab men came over to his one-bedroom property on the ground floor, and took up an alarming stance, sullenly surrounding him as he sat on his garden chair.

They all wore expensive dark sunglasses, and his rheumy eyes couldn't see their features properly, under their cotton-white head coverings.

The taxi driver wiped his mouth carefully, not too worried yet at the overcrowding of his space. He spoke in the Arab tongue. "Can I help you, gentlemen? Do you require my services?"

One of the Arab's answered him. "No, not yet. We are trying to trace a friend who took a ride somewhere in your taxi. We need to know where you took him."

"Today, or yesterday?" The old man asked politely, shielding his eyes from the wicked glare of the sun. He had meant to move his chair further back under the awning once he'd finished eating.

"Today. Late morning. Did you go over the Al Maqtaa Bridge?"

"Ah, I have been very busy traveling here and there! I have been picking up people the whole morning, wanting me to drive them to Al Maqtaa! You will have to describe this friend."

"He's male, medium height, with a bald head, and a lean beard! You must remember him, surely?"

"I don't know..."

"Cast your mind back, old man! Our friend was wearing casual European clothes, and he's a white man!"

"Ah! White, you say? I'm still not sure! We have many foreign tourists visit here! It's hard to remember..."

"Perhaps this will jog your memory!" One of the three impatient Arabs had drawn a flick-knife from his pocket. He opened it threateningly.

The taxi driver gazed at the sharp point in amazement, sensing now these were no ordinary questions! He looked alarmed, and shrank away from the blade.

"I tell you, I can't remember this man! I am only a poor taxi driver! Please, I beg you, do not use that infernal weapon on me!"

"Perhaps you will remember your tips? Were any higher than usual?"

"S-some! I carry millionaires to their destinations as well, you know? But I still can't –"

The Arab bounded close beside the old man, holding the flick-knife to his throat.

"You must think harder, or you will die, friend!"

"G-give me a moment! I can't think with that in my face!" The old man begged. His pale lips moved silently as if he was praying to Allah. Then, he clicked his fingers, his heavily lined eyes lighting up with hopeful inspiration.

"There was a man with a bald head! I saw him come out of a property near Premier Inn, and he hailed me!"

"But that isn't in the Al Maqtaa sector! It's near the airport!"

Frightened now, the old man groaned. "I'm sure it was the Inn beside the airport! I definitely drove him away from it!"

"Is that all you remember?" The other man's voice was low and dangerous. "Then where did you take him?"

"Wait!" The old man screeched in alarm as the knife moved towards him. He shook his ghutra covered head. "I swear by Allah, I can't remember! I think we did drive near the Al Maqtaa sector, but I didn't take him near the bridge!

He wanted me to drive him all over the place! I'm not sure where we went!" He finished lamely, eyeing the flick-knife as if it was a venomous snake.

"You are a useless, foolish old man! We may return! If we do – try to remember your contacts next time!"

With this curt warning, thankfully, the Arabs left him – a deadly-frightened old man, shaking as if with the ague. It was a long time before he roused himself from his garden chair to unsteadily pour himself a much-needed stiff drink from a new bottle of brandy!

# LONDON. A LONG WAIT

Paul Wright had spent a restless night waiting for a call from Leigh's kidnappers. When Serena called him at four that morning he thought it would be them, and having at last got her off the line, he waited and waited for news of his daughter, wondering where the hell had Silverman got to?

The man was an enigma, a law unto himself, Paul thought. He'd only hired him a month ago, when a few days before this had come the first warning of someone trying to take Leigh.

On an early evening in June, a light-footed brown-skinned man, swathed European-style in a belted black raincoat, wearing a bulgy woolen black hat that obscured most of his face, had attempted to knife Leigh's chauffeur when he'd opened her door to let her out of the family car. (She wasn't driving at the time as she hadn't passed her test). This had happened at Paul Wright's country retreat in Hereford. Leigh's shocked scream alerted her chauffeur, and with quick presence of mind, he managed to fight off his assailant, yelling for help from those working late in the stables, and the attacker had retreated, slipping away through the wooded undergrowth that marked the borders of Paul Wright's large estate.

The police were called. A hasty search of Paul's estate yielded that a light aircraft of some kind had landed in a nearby field, unseen, and shielded by trees. Whether this had been the 'getaway' machine was anyone's guess. It must have flown low, or been designed with non-metallic composites and fuselage as it hadn't been noted on radar. Police had been unable to trace or track its origins.

No Flying School had reported a missing plane stolen from their airfields.

A gauze pad and syringe filled with a liquid solution of

Temazepam had been found lying, dropped quickly on the driveways tarmacadam. No fingerprints were found.

A concerned Paul had immediately brought his daughter to London, where he could keep an eye on her. She had been shaken back then, in June, but had passed the incident off lightly afterwards with the vigor of the young, as London life, meeting her debutante friends at glamorous, notorious dress parties, night clubbing in the capital, and enjoying a quick, secretly-arranged wild holiday abroad, took over.

Paul had gratefully paid his chauffeur generous money for fighting his attacker and saving his devoted only daughter from possible kidnap. The man accepted his money but left soon after, preferring to work for a safer employee.

Paul decided his daughter needed a minder. Someone who could shadow her well, and who worked discreetly, reporting to him whatever she did.

Silverman had fitted the bill. Paul took him on little realizing he was a special Operative working for an elite police department. All he knew was that Silverman worked precisely and quietly, which comforted Paul's worried heart. He had been recommended to Paul by a friend's friend, Jack Ashcombe, who was an ex-CID operative who Paul only knew through Ben Elliston. Ben Elliston was an MP friend of Paul's and the two men often dined at their London club together. Elliston's flat was only a few blocks from where Paul lived.

Still thinking all this Paul jumped when his mobile rang again. Could this be the kidnappers at last?

His hands were clammy with sweat as he fumbled to pick it up, trying to place his reading glasses on his nose at the same time...

# NEARING ABU DHABI.
# OBEYING ORDERS

The Arab with his gun pointed it at both girls, speaking slowly in English: "We shall arrive within the next hour. You are being asked to put on these clothes over what you are already wearing."

The other Arab who had served them food entered, and had something black folded over his arm. He threw the black stuff onto one of the bunk-beds.

"W-where are we?" Leigh asked tremulously, eyeing the gun owlishly, as if she didn't believe this was happening to her.

"It is not necessary that you know this."

"But you've kidnapped us, haven't you? We need to know where you're taking us!"

"Quiet! Put the clothes on, NOW!"

"Better do as he says, Leigh." Fran hesitantly touched her friend's arm.

"Oh, all right! But there's so many questions I need to ask, and their not telling us!"

"Perhaps they don't know..." Fran picked up what looked like an all-in-one black robe and struggled into it.

Leigh did the same. Their robes touched the floor, and they found to their surprise that they could only see out of the garment through narrow oblong slits!

"Christ! What is this thing?" Leigh asked. "I feel like I'm invisible, or something."

"It's stifling, whatever it is." Fran answered. "Have you noticed the heat? It's got very hot all of a sudden!"

Seeing they were ready, the Arab with the gun beckoned them towards the opening he and his partner had entered by. He spoke a warning. "We are moving you to the center of the jet where it is cool. Do not attempt to escape. We will be watching you!"

Through the eye slit in their garments they saw him tap his gun. Frightened still, they had no choice but to obey him.

They walked through a split curtain to find themselves in the long, narrow lounge area of what seemed like a compact, private jet-plane. There was an open cockpit ahead, but their long, stiff robes and their awkward eye-slits prevented them from seeing the pilot properly.

It was definitely cooler in the jet's lounge, which consisted of a round white table, and four large white comfortable leather swivel chairs bolted to the thick, stuck-down carpeted floor. Blinds were drawn over most of the portholes to give minimal shade from the blaring sun.

"I bid you sit." The Arab with the gun indicated the chairs. "If you try to move from these you will be tied again. Belt yourselves in tightly, there will be some turbulence when we try to land."

Silent now, the girls obeyed him, and once seated, strapped themselves into their chairs.

Satisfied they were restrained and still, the two Arabs sat down in the remaining chairs and proceeded to play foreign games on their mobiles. The man with the gun kept it ready beside his hand on the table, as he stabbed with pleasure at his Smart phone.

Fran found Leigh's hand and they held on tightly, whilst anxious thoughts on their demise swirled around in their tense, worried minds.

The small, private jet droned on to its destination carrying its stricken cargo.

# THE FORCES HOTEL,
# ABU DHABI. DIFFICULT DECISIONS

Aware something was wrong, Derrick watched the shock on Karl's face turn to anxiety.

He heard Karl say: "I bet they've been taken to a remote corner of England! I need to come back and help them, but I can't be in two places at once! This damn news upsets all my plans!"

The soothing man's voice on the other end replied: "Don't worry Karl, there's nothing you can do here. Leave it to us! We're on the job, and we'll tackle it for you!"

"I must come back! I don't like the idea they're in danger because of me!"

"As said, we'll sort it."

"The man I'm after is crafty, greedy for money, and ambitious! He'll stop at nothing to cover himself! How could he learn so much about me? I was cautious when I asked the Abu Dhabi police to spy on his dealings! They already have a file on him, but can't prove how corrupt he is!"

"That is why you're out there, Karl. Don't worry about your women friends, we'll find them!"

"Sod it! My plans may have to be altered! Don't let any harm come to my friends, will you? I'm really distraught by this unsettling news! I wish I could return to help you search!"

"I give you my word we'll do everything we can this end. Keep us informed of your plans. Good luck!"

Karl switched off his mobile, and rubbed his jaw anxiously. He caught Derrick's eye and spoke shortly: "The man I'm after has a hold on me! I underestimated his actions!"

"How do you mean? What's happened to upset you so forcibly, Karl?"

"I helped a Croatian lady and her daughter settle in England. I hear from CIUSO that they've both been abducted!"

"Good God! Whatever for?"

"Because the man who's ordered this devious intervention is warning me not to interfere in his affairs – he knows I'm here! I suspected it, as I was followed earlier – and did nothing about it. My friends, Tanja and Kimmi are now in grave danger because of my stupidity! I should have captured the man tracking me and asked questions of him, even 'though I covered my real destination purposes when I arrived here!"

"That's terrible! But you're not to blame! You couldn't have known what he was planning? How are you going to manage now? What will you do?"

"Nothing! I have to damn-well stay here, carry on with this mission against my will! It's a sod of a dilemma!"

Derrick said simply: "I'm sorry. Are CIUSO helping in any way?"

"Yeah – the guys are sorting this out, but I want to be there, to help Tanja and Kimmi! We had an argument before I left England; Tanja asked me to live with her, and I said I couldn't, I didn't want her and the child placed in any kind of danger because of my job. You know how it is, Dickie?"

"Ye-es, when I worked for CIUSO, it wasn't as an operative, only an adviser... I didn't consider my job to be as dangerous as yours. But I see what you mean! It isn't wise to advertise your family and friends so openly in your line of business! I live near my son since my wife died, but I still put his interests before mine. You do when you have family! This crooked dealer has definitely put you on the spot! Obviously, you must try and carry on! I think its imperative that you get to this wicked crook first! Can I help in any way?"

Karl smiled wanly. "Having you listen to my problems is good enough, Dickie! But, that's my aim – to get there first! If all works well, tonight will be important. I can't really change my plans now!"

Derrick leaned forward, repeating himself again. "What will you do?"

"I'll have to think quickly!" Karl replied, grimly.

# LONDON. STILL WAITING

"Hi, Paul, it's Ben Elliston here. How are you? Not at work today?"

"Oh, it's you, Ben! I suppose I'm okay, but I don't work Saturdays, unless I have to! Er, what can I do for you?"

"I was wondering if you fancied a round of golf?"

"Golf? No thanks Ben, I'm a bit tied up right now."

"Not 'tied up' literally! You sound tired, not overdoing checking all the overdrafts and business rates?"

"No, nothing like that! I really wish it was, I wouldn't be hanging around like this, dragging my heels on the floor –"

"You sound pensive, Paul. What's bugging you?"

"Ben, I'm fine." Paul spoke flatly.

"I'm not convinced; you don't sound like yourself at all. Forgive me if I'm intruding, but is your ex-wife causing grief again?"

Paul groaned loudly, and Ben heard him.

"I'm right! She's nothing but trouble for you! Confounded woman!"

"It-it's not Serena, Ben, it's Leigh –!

"Leigh? Why, what's she done?"

"She hasn't done anything, except be ki –"

"Except, what? Is she all right? You're not making much sense!"

Paul sighed again, raising his eyes to the ceiling. "Look, Ben, can you keep a secret?"

"I'm – of course I can, man, what's wrong?"

He heard the deep, unsteady breath Paul took before he explained curtly: "Leigh's been kidnapped!"

"Good God! Not again? How do you know this?"

Paul told the MP jerkily, what had happened last night.

Ben listened, then said: "So Jack Ashcombe's man was hired by you! I was going to ask you whether you took this Silverman character on, to safeguard Leigh? He seems an efficient, steady, secretive sort!"

"But he doesn't want me to call the police," Paul wailed.

"And do you?"

"In my heart – yes! I feel I should do something, but Silverman claims he can handle this. By Christ – I'm putting a lot of trust in that man!"

"I see your dilemma... Perhaps you should call the police? Go against Silverman's orders?"

"I'm still waiting for Silverman, or them, to call me, but no one's contacted me yet. I've not slept, nor eaten since midnight, when he broke the awful news to me!"

"Do you want me to come round? I could whip you up a meal?"

"Er, no thanks, not yet. I need to stay here!"

"Of course, friend! But you'd feel better after some hot food and drink! Let me come over?"

"After the kidnapper's phone call." Paul was adamant. "I must be patient and wait, they, or Silverman will be in touch!"

"Hmm, very well. Good luck, then, Paul. I'll wait 'till I hear from you, okay?"

"Okay – and, Ben?"

"What?"

"If you go to the club today, don't say anything to anyone!"

"As you wish. Remember, I'm here to help. Take care, Paul."

"Yeah, thanks." Paul hung up.

Ben Elliston also hung up, but a few seconds later he was making another call...

# ABU DHABI. DELIVERY PLANS

"I am not going to wear that over my face!" Despite the gun threat Leigh was kicking her heels in. She pointed to the dark veil that was held in the man's hand who had fed them earlier.

"It is a gishwa. It is traditional to cover your eyes here." Spoke the Arab with the gun calmly.

"Where is 'here'?"

"We are flying over Dubai."

"Dubai? Christ, but that's –"

"In the United Arab Emirates."

"Arab? My God – we're in Arabia! Jesus Christ, I just do not believe it! What the shit are we doing here?"

"Oh, bloody hell!" Echoed Fran in total horror, when she heard this. "These clothes –?"

"You are wearing a niquab. It is a traditional docile garment for the women of our country who do not want foreign eyes staring at them, and to ward off unsavory male advances."

"I think I'm going to faint!" Fran gasped. She grabbed Leigh's arm unsteadily. "How in God's name have we ended up here? I just want to go home!" She began to cry, which made her mascara run and her eyes smart.

"Now look what you've done!" Leigh intoned rebelliously. "You've upset my friend – and me!"

To her amazement she was deliberately ignored. "Are you both deaf? I said –"

The gun was wielded before her startled eyes. "This is a warning – make no mistake, we give the orders here!"

Fran placed a tentative hand on her friends arm. "I'm fine now. We'd better do as we're told, Leigh!"

Leigh looked mutinously at the gun, and muttered:

"God, I hate all this! Who do they think they are?"

"Come," said the man with the gun, waving it impatiently. "Put the gishwa on now! We have no time to lose. There is more travel yet, by car, and it is very hot outside."

Both girls were still upset, but Leigh allowed the Arab with the gun to escort her to an old white land rover, waiting alongside the very light Honda Jet with its engine ticking over. Squinting at the land rover's dust-streaked dirty windows, they could just make out a blurred image of their Arab driver, waiting patiently for them to clamber into their outdated mode of transport.

An ocean of reddish-gold sand lay all around them as far as the eye could see, due to feldspar in the soil, with some very fantastically-high, wind-blown sand dunes. The wilderness area they were in seemed otherworldly to the frightened girls. If they hadn't been so hot and sweaty they would have shivered in fear at being in these barren, hostile surroundings. As soon as they all got into the car they saw the pilot in the cockpit start his engines, and the light, nimble private jet taxied away down the flat, grainy disused track they were standing on, without sinking into the wallowing sand, ready for take-off.

"Where are we going?" Leigh asked stoutly.

"Be quiet! You will soon find out."

"I might run away, yell for help in the desert!" Leigh warned.

"You cannot run far! And you would find no-one to aid you! Rub'al-Khali desert is the hottest on earth, large and very deadly! Left out in the open under this scorching sun, you would die before evening without water! At night you would shiver with cold and catch hypothermia, and could be stung by poisonous insects! There are no man-made Oasis's here!"

At this startling report, Leigh groaned and clamped her mouth shut. But she muttered venomously under her breath: "I hope your oil wells dry up soon, you waspy thug!" Hearing this Fran looked even more worried and scared, thinking the Arab might hear her friend, and shoot them down there and then!

The Arab with the gun who had told them about the heat outside, had been right about it. Huddled inside their niquabs, the girls were wilting in the back of the dirty land rover, despite the car's antique air-conditioning.

They realized they were enduring the merciless, sweltering heat of the desert. It seemed like they'd both stepped back in time to an ancient land of forbidding majesty, mysterious and empty. They saw a carpet of wind-whipped sand swirling and undulating like ice-cream pouring from a tap, under the brazen sun, piling into beautiful crescent shapes, and beyond, an endless ocean of red-gold grains stretching towards the heat-fazed hazy horizon. Trying to watch this glaring expanse of sand from the car's open window made the girls eyes water. They did not see the beauty of the dunes, to them this wide, shimmering and alien landscape seemed the most unforgiving in the world! And there were no signposts!

There was nothing to see but rolling golden-red desert with massive areas of flat land, and those fantastic sculptured sand dunes piled high upon each other, forever shifting and moving under a relentless dry wind.

The bumpy old land rover followed an open dusty track through kilometers of endless sand, before stopping at a disused well. The wind and sand had eroded its sides so that it looked like a melting wall of half-baked rubble, it's jagged circumference broken into dust, its waters run dry, as void of life as the surrounding desert. Waiting beside the well was an elegant cherry-colored, brand new Bentley Mulsanne. The girls were ordered out of the old range rover and into the new, plush car, which soon turned onto a modern highway, zooming along it, easily eating up the kilometers. After roughly what seemed an hour's time, in the shimmering distance the girls could faintly make out a horizon of shining sun-kissed skyscrapers, plushly and partly hidden by a wall of lush green trees.

Tense, without realizing it, they held each others hot

hands again, for reassurance. The heat was terrible and both felt faint, and sick with fear. Soon, they would know their fate.

# ABU DHABI, THE FORCE'S HOTEL. WORRIES.

Having already given his earlier orders to a reluctant Rachid, Karl decided he'd go ahead with his plans, but this latest predicament, and his worry over Tanja and Kimmi's safety weighed him down.

Trying to help, Derrick suggested to Karl that he stay at this hotel for the duration of his visit. He assured Karl it was 'most suitable'. It was a five star hotel in the Al Maqtaa sector. The reception was open 24 hours and Karl went there and signed in. In his room, when he was led to it, he found it had internet connection. Sixty minutes of free Wi-Fi, then a state-chosen advert, then another sixty minutes of more free Wi-Fi which he didn't need, as he used his special phone for 'the den' boys to make contact with. He also had a mini drinks bar in his room. Most guests staying at hotels could now buy drinks, and even casual visitors to hotels were allowed to order a drink at the bar. It was considered sinful for Muslims to drink excessive alcohol. They needed a license to drink – even at home. They could also quench their thirst in 'liquor shops', or western hotels that provided a room for them to relax, smoke and drink in, especially during Ramadan.

There was also a nearby beach, and not far away, was the stunning, majestic, towering Sheikh Zayed Grand Mosque, which you could visit, and get an idea of the country's culture. Not that he would have time to go sight-seeing, although he'd been here before, on a short mission. There were places to tour that were on his wish list. He had hoped he might one day, swim in the net-fenced-off sea with the whale sharks, the spotted rays, and trigger fish, and maybe, even spot an elephant calf! But now wasn't the time, there was too much at stake. Karl's mind churned over his extra worry and plans. More alert than ever, he wasn't leaving anything to chance, now he had the true measure of the man he was after.

Karl left Derrick and went to his room for a catnap, with tough thoughts spinning in his head. But, first, using his special CIUSO connection card, he sent a text message from his mobile to somewhere in England over a secure connection. Then he called Paul Wright.

Paul answered on the first ring. "Yes?"

"It's Silverman. Have they called yet?"

Paul said, bluntly: "Not yet, the blighters! I'm peeing my pants waiting!"

"They will make contact soon, when the girls have been taken to their destination."

"How do you know all this?"

"I've had experience before."

"Where are you anyway?"

Karl told him and Paul's thin brown eyebrows shot upwards.

"You're saying my only daughter is somewhere in the bloody Emirates? Oh, my poor darling! What a shock for her! So far from home –" Paul's voice broke. Sensing some inconsolable gut-feeling of abject despair, in panic, he ordered urgently. "Get her out of there, Silverman! Get her out! I'll pay you double your wage, but get her out!"

"I'm working on it. I'll call again – soon. Goodbye."

Paul was left holding his mobile with a dead connection. He sat down on his chair and sniffed loudly. A few worried tears for Leigh gathered in his eyes, and he squeezed them shut, moaning to himself. Dear Christ, let her please be all right!

Karl set the alarm on his mobile for an hour's sleep, and lay on the comfy king-sized hotel bed, half naked, purposefully stilling his mind to alpha rhythm through silent meditation, as he had been taught by a group of Shaolin monks.

He managed to sleep, despite his worries over Tanja and Kimmi. Where were they now?

# SATURDAY. SHUT IN

For the umpteenth time, Tanja banged wildly on the locked ply-wood door separating her from their kidnappers. If they were in the next room, they didn't answer her. She gave up and turned to her wide-eyed daughter, shrugging angrily, and spoke soothingly in the Croatian tongue. She had taught Kimmi English, but the young child hadn't quite mastered it yet, and it was easier, in her anger, to slip back into her own language.

"Don't worry, sweetheart, they must have gone out! I expect they'll be back later. We'll have to wait for them to return and, hopefully, let us go!"

"Mummy, why are we here?"

"I think it might be to do with uncle Karl's work... It's best not to mention him to these men, okay?"

Kimmi nodded solemnly. "Will uncle Karl come and get us out? I don't like it here! I'm scared! They scared me!"

Tanja's mind whirled back, remembering how they'd been taken by surprise this Saturday morning, at her apartment. She and Kimmi had risen later than usual, as Tanja hadn't had to go to work at the coffee-shop until 10 am, and she'd planned to take her child to work with her. Kostas didn't mind, he liked children. She grimaced at the memory of the two, big white men in casual street clothes, who had burst into her bedroom to find her and Kimmi playing with the child's toys together. Thankfully, she and Kimmi had both been fully dressed. There hadn't even been time to scream; both of them were whisked away, with the men's hands covering their mouths, half man-handled, half carried down their five steps to a waiting car, which screeched off quickly through the London streets.

Tanja had struggled wildly, her heartbeat choking her, wanting to get her daughter away from the other man's clutches, but the unknown man dragging her along with him was stronger than she.

As soon as she had been unceremoniously dumped in the back of the car, with Kimmi beside her, she'd cried out fearfully: "Who are you? Why have you done this? What do you want with us?"

"Shut up, Miss Kovacevic! You'll figure it out! Our boss has been told by another party to have the pair of you taken somewhere!"

"Why?"

"Because of your boyfriend!"

"I haven't got a boyfriend! There's been some mistake! Where are we going?"

"Nowhere you need to worry about! Now, keep your mouth zipped, lady!"

Thinking this, Tanja choked down her anger and spoke soothingly to her frightened child. "I know they did, darling. It's fine, mummy's with you! I won't let anyone harm you!"

She crossed the bulb-lit empty box room they'd been put in and hugged her daughter to her protectively, wondering herself if Karl would hear of this, and come and rescue them. She didn't know he'd traveled through the very early morning to Abu Dhabi.

In the meantime, they would have to wait. She sighed impatiently, gently stroking her daughter's long hair.

# LONDON. DOUBTS

"That's funny," Mandy Tompkins put the hall phone receiver back on its stand, "I can't get hold of Fran."

Her husband Nigel was in the kitchen, reading his paper. He shouted out: "She's probably gone shopping."

"Well, no. She was supposed to come round to me this morning, to take me shopping!"

"Bet she's forgotten, love! Else she's still in bed! Didn't she say she had to go out late last night? Something to do with work?"

"That's right. She's still asleep then. I'll ring her later on, I've got all day, I can wait!"

As she finished speaking, the phone rang.

"It's probably her now! Hello?"

"Mrs. Tompkins?"

"Yes?"

"Hi, I'm Isobelle, Fran's flatmate. I didn't know if Fran was staying with you or not?"

"No. Fran's not here, dear. I thought she was at the flat?"

"No, she's not. I'm a nurse, and when I came in from my shift just now, I saw that Fran's bed hadn't been slept in. So I thought she was with you!"

"Oh dear, she's not here! I wonder where she can be? She was coming over to me today."

"Then she's probably on her way to you. Sorry for bothering, but I thought it unusual her bed hasn't been slept in."

"She had to go out late last night. Perhaps, like you, she hasn't come back yet? I'll hang on a bit longer, in case she's on her way. Thanks for your concern!"

"Okay, thought I'd ring in case she was home! Bye!"

# ABU DHABI. THE PENTHOUSE

The skyscrapers of Abu Dhabi were high and magnificent, block after block, some designed in terracotta and dune concrete, glass and steel, in superb modern styles, their windows gleaming and polished in the hot sun. Spectacular Minarets and Mosques slid-by in side roads near the skyscrapers, and through their veils, the girls glimpsed flamboyant souks (or rambling markets), as the luxuriant and stylish Bentley Mulsanne flashed past. Glossy and elegant, sculptured Abu Dhabi looked vibrant, full of life and color.

From what they could see through their Arab uniforms both girls were awed by its splendor. The shiny skyscrapers spoke of profound business transactions, finance, banking and luxury apartments; the white, gold, silver-colored domed embellished Mosques spoke of prayer, of hidden, ancient Islamic traditions, and the souks displayed rich pickings and bargains galore for the unwary tourist.

Then they drew up outside a long square, moderate, three-story hotel and their heartbeat quickened. Their driver past the swish cars in the parking lot and swung into a dark passageway that led into a paved forecourt with a fountain spraying water and the slogan 'PRIVATE' etched on a gilt decorated wooden stake.

"Out now." Said the Arab with the gun, and the girls had to obey.

"Act docile, or you will be shot!"

The girls followed the one who had fed them, their legs stiff and sweaty from the car ride, despite the Mulsannes apparent comfort and cool air control. It was difficult not to bump into this Arab with their face-masks on. The man made straight for the back of the hotel, and led the girls through an open door and down a passageway. Cool air hit them in the face, for the air conditioners were on full blast.

It was a welcome relief. They saw no one.

The other man followed behind them, with his hand in his pocket, pointing it at the girls as they walked self-consciously towards a lift, which lay adjacent to the back entrance of the hotel, at the end of the corridor.

They all filed into the lift, and the man who had fed them thumbed a button on the wall, entitled with the word 'Penthouse' in English, followed by a flourish of Arabic symbols.

It took them up to the 4th floor, which was slightly higher than the main hotel block, where the doors rolled back, and the girls found themselves in a square red-painted hall.

"Wait here!" Hissed the man with the gun. "I will tell our master you have arrived! He is dying to see you!" He chuckled. "You can take the gishwas and the niquabs off now."

"But we're not properly dressed! I'm only wearing a thin frock, so is Fran!"

"It matters little whether you are dressed or bare!" Came the chilling answer.

Leigh glanced at Fran. "I think I prefer this ancient old garb!"

"Me, too." Fran agreed. "I'm not going through that door in the nude! Whatever do they take us for!"

"Enough! You must wear what you wore when we found you! Or my master will have you both shot!"

Resigned, the girls took off their outer garments. The other Arab picked up their discarded robes.

"There!" Leigh glared at both Arabs. "Satisfied?"

The Arab with the gun nodded. He knocked on a fiery red engraved wooden double door, and a cultured voice from within called out: "Enter!"

They all filed into a big white room filled with lazy beams of sunlight, escaping like coiled tendrils from behind shaded blinds. The intense gleam of the white walls dazzled the girls eyes, and for a moment they couldn't see the slightly thick-set man sitting on a curbed white sofa eyeing their intrepid entry with a triumphant, smug grin.

He wore a long loose white robe. His teeth were as white as the sofa and his hair, wavy and jet black, had no gray. He was handsome in a dark, dusky way, with sardonic brown eyes under craggy, prominent bushy eyebrows. He flapped a languid hand at the man with the gun, and it looked as if his fingernails had been gently manicured — even painted in see-through gloss.

As he stood up, the robe revealed itself to be a kandura, or thobe — a flowing garment that many Arab men wore in the hot summer months. He was not wearing any form of Arab headdress such as the ghutrah. It was just too hot.

"So, my packages have arrived!"

"We're not packages – we're people!" Leigh was stung into announcing hotly.

The man laughed. "Forgive my manners, you are my English packages!"

"We're people." Leigh spoke firmly, her chin up, but quivering slightly.

"Well – people, welcome to Abu Dhabi. I don't suppose you've been here before?" He addressed Leigh, ignoring Fran completely. She was looking distressed and tired from the heat.

Leigh, on guard and tense, shook her head mutely.

The man continued smoothly. "It is an exceptional, magical city. Here, you can have whatever you wish for."

"Then I wish for a magic carpet to spirit me and my friend home, away from you!"

"Now, now, Leigh, isn't it? You are very like a woman I know – you always find an answer, don't you? Unlike your friend, who seems a little quiet!"

He moved to Fran's side and trickled his fingers familiarly through her uncombed long blond tresses. Her diamanté designed clasp was no longer in her hair, she'd lost it since last night's hasty abduction. She pulled back from him immediately, like a frightened rabbit.

"Leave Fran alone!"

"But she is with you, and she will be treated the same way as you. It is something you will have to get used to here. We find blond-haired women fascinating!"

Both girls fidgeted uneasily after this speech.

Leigh asked, tremulously: "Who are you that you kidnap us like this?"

"I am Asad Boulos. My first name means 'lion' in Arabic, and I am the 'king' of this domain. I am a prosperous man, and own this hotel. It is all mine!"

"Why have we been kidnapped?" Leigh tried to find answers from this enigmatic, conceited Arab. "My father will be very worried when he learns I didn't come home last night!"

"And my parents will be worrying, too!" Put in Fran, suddenly finding her voice, which sounded strained and squeaky.

Asad ignored Fran and answered Leigh curtly. "Yes. Your father is also rich! Need you ask why the kidnap, when, at the end of the day, it boils down to money, eh?"

"You greedy pig!"

Asad's grin changed to a frown. "I will not be called names! I could have you whipped for insolence! But you do not know the rules of my country! We do not bow to any man except Allah. Like-wise, I do not bow to you! You are below my station. So I accept your insulting ignorance towards me! I am the master here, and my men, Emir and Ameen, know this. You will know this also, for I now control your destinies. Your friend for instance, there are many sex dealers in other countries that would give me good money for her."

"You can't do that!" Gasped Leigh. "You mustn't send her away from me! I-I need her to be with me – we're almost like sisters! Oh please! Don't send her to sex dealers! I-I'll obey you, if that's what you want?"

"You have, what do they say, 'changed your tune'? That is better! Now, my men will look after you whilst I go about my business. I will be contacting your father shortly, and I will need you with me!" He pointed to Leigh. "Emir,

Ameen? Find these people some refreshment and show them to their room. Farewell, for now!"

Emir walked up to the girls who were looking nonplussed, dejected and worn-out.

"This way. There will be refreshment for you shortly."

Once again, the bewildered girls followed the two Arab men from the large room to a smaller one, on the other side of the red-painted hallway.

"You can wash and change in here." Emir opened the wooden, single carved door, and the girls entered a room of reasonable size which had two single beds in it, both draped in white satin duvets. There was an open wardrobe nearby, filled with women's burqa's, abaya's and niquabs in various sizes and colours.

Emir, who seemed to be the spokesman of the two, said patiently: "Choose a garment, any one. You can wash in the adjoining bathroom. Ameen will bring you food and drink."

"I want a vodka – for my nerves!" Leigh flashed at him.

"Later, you may. For now, you must drink coffee. It will refresh you! Ameen will knock on the door when you have finished, but we shall lock you in!"

"Oh no! Not more captivity!"

"It is a precaution. I leave you now."

"Oh, God!" Leigh sat down opposite a long dressing-table ledge, that had a wide mirror fastened to the wall. She ignored her hot, pale reflection and placed her head in her arms, wailing: "I want to go home!"

"I know!" Fran put her arms around the taller girl and gave her a hug. "So do I, but we must do as they say for the time being! We'd better try these clothes on. I feel exposed with this dress cut so low!"

"So do I. When he said that, about women with blond hair, I wanted to cut mine off, just to spite him!"

"Yes, I understand. He's an arrogant bugger!"

Ameen brought them coffee with some kind of Arabian stew. The girls ate it automatically, as it was the only thing to do! The stew tasted exquisite and expensive, and on any other occasion they might have enjoyed it, but not today. Their perilous plight worried them.

Then, dressed in a white abaya, Leigh was called away to contact her father. Fran sat on her bed and twiddled her thumbs, thinking about herself, and anxiously wondering how her parents were coping. They would know by now that something was wrong! Asad Boulos hadn't even mentioned them; he was concentrating on Leigh's father, not her people! A cold feeling flooded Fran's stomach. Leigh was the important one, she was only a gatecrasher! Whatever would they do to her? She felt powerless and alone.

# ABU DHABI. DISTRESS CALL

"Dad? Daddy, get me out of here, please! Pay what he wants, but get me out – I can't stand it!"

The mobile was taken from her abruptly. Leigh hadn't meant to break down, but the long flight, the heat, the shock of being in a foreign country among hostile strangers sporting guns had proved too much for her anxious nerves, and she'd blabbered into the mouthpiece at her father like a fourteen year old school kid unexpectedly expelled from school!

Paul had been in his modern kitchen eating dry, left-over canapes from the day before, and drinking alternate cups of coffee and whiskey when his mobile rang. He nearly scalded himself with the hot coffee as he quickly reached for it.

"Yes?"

Then he heard his daughter's anguished voice and he shouted into the mouthpiece: "Leigh! Leigh – I'm here, darling! Are you all right? They haven't harmed you?"

His disappointment went deep when his questions were answered by a foreigners cultured voice.

"Mr Wright, I have your daughter, and you have proof she has spoken to you. Now, she is all right, but if you do not pay the price I ask, you will never see your daughter again! Is that clear?"

Paul answered curtly, grating his teeth. "Crystal clear, yes!"

"I want a vast sum of money from you. It must be administered by wire transfer to a certain off-shore account. Again, do you understand what I ask from you?"

"Yes, you bugger, I do. How much?"

The voice at the other end of the line named a price

which set Paul reeling.

"I can't give you that amount!"

"If you want your daughter back safe and sound, you can. It's your choice, Mr Wright. Remember this message to stir your senses: nor the moon by night shall see them ever again! I mean this! It is my favorite warning!" The line went dead.

# ABU DHABI.
# A MEETING IN THE DESERT

Karl woke to the sound of his mobile's alarm beeping. After only a half-hour's catnap he was instantly alert, his mind racing, remembering Tanja and Kimmi's predicament. He rinsed his face and hands in cold water from the adjoining wash-room, had a quick shave, brushed his teeth, and pulled on his packed shorts and blue polo shirt, then picked up his cap and new sunglasses. He swung his Nike gym bag on his shoulder and was ready to go.

Messages on his mobile could wait. Karl wanted to see how Rachid had got on with the mission he'd sent him on.

He found Rachid in the smoker's den, his hunched back standing out from those seated, smoking nearby. Derrick was also still sitting in his armchair in the bar area, reading an English newspaper. Karl steered Rachid over to Derrick's table. The ex squadron leader was pleased to see them again.

Karl beamed a genuine smile at him, then turned to Rachid and asked: "Well, Rachid, how did you get on? Did you find out anything interesting from the gentleman I sent you in search of?"

Rachid gave a deep smile of contentment. "Ah, he flickered like a flame when I mentioned his bastard son! Very prickly at first, but he admitted his indiscretions in the end!"

"So I was right! Asad is his son?"

"Sadly, it appears so. I tell you, Farid Al Ghazzawi was very, very angry, and inflamed by what his crooked son has attempted to do!"

"Does that mean that Al Ghazzawi is on our side?"

"He was angry enough to appear to be. He says Asad is

debouching the Bedouin way of life and he cannot forgive him! He will meet you. I have arranged this."

"Soon?"

"Soon, Mr Karl. We are to meet in the desert, at one of the old Bedouin camps. I know where it is and I can drive you to it!"

Karl turned to Derrick. "Dickie, you said you were feeling tired, but if you're up to it, would you like to come with us for a desert visit? It would make a break from sitting here all day!"

Derrick's green eyes shone. He nodded. "I'm not so tired now. I'd love to, but is there a special reason why you want me to come with you?"

Karl grinned. "Yes, to keep our Bedouin friend, Al Ghazzawi sweet. I want him to think we are acting on a noble impulse! His help will be a bonus for my plan, and you're a good 'people's' mediator whom I'd be proud to have on my team!"

At that moment Karl's mobile rang. He answered quickly: "Yes, Paul?"

"I've been contacted. The swine I spoke to says I'll never see Leigh again, unless I pay their ransom demand. It's damn sickening! I want to do something to help her rather than sitting here twiddling my bloody thumbs!"

"Believe me, I understand that! How much are they asking?"

Paul told him and Karl whistled. "Have you got that amount?"

"In my stocks and shares, just about, and the monies I drew from the bank earlier. They want it in American dollars by wire transfer. It may take me some time to draw out all this and place in my personal account! Silverman, do you know where their holding my daughter?"

"I've a shrewd idea... Don't worry, I'll work on it!"

"Can I call the police?"

"No! No police, yet. I have good reasons for not involving them!"

"Er, I've told one of my friends."

"You shouldn't have done that!"

"I had to tell someone!"

"Who?"

"Ben Elliston, the MP."

Karl groaned. "Damn! I've heard of him! Look – I know how you feel, but I don't need extra complications right now! You must trust me!"

There was an exasperated sigh at the other end.

Karl took a breath. "I'll call when I've news. Try not to worry." He clicked his phone off grimly and spoke to the listening Rachid: "When do we meet our honored Bedouin friend?"

Rachid squinted at his cheap watch. "We go now, in my old jalopy. Have you a gun, because you might need it! I don't trust desert pirates or Bedu's!"

Karl grinned. "I have a gun! Why don't you trust Bedouin's?"

"Because they are squatters residing on State Land! Some can be dangerous! If they all mass together, they could become a security threat to our country, if they chose to!"

Karl shook his head ruefully. "I don't think so! There are not enough of them now who still reside in the desert! Most seem to live in allotted homes and flats, not tents any more!"

"Are you expecting any violence?" Asked Derrick, slightly alarmed, although he was looking forward to a desert ride!

"Don't worry, I won't allow harm to come to you, Dickie! It's just a precaution! Nothing we can't handle, eh Rachid?"

Rachid looked surly. "Don't count me in, Mr Karl – I'm only the driver!"

There was such a dismal look on Rachid's face that Derrick laughed gleefully. He was in his element, helping Karl, and feeling needed again. It was a blissful, wonderful moment for him.

# ABU DHABI. SMOOTHING THE WAY

Asad called Serena at her small apartment from his Penthouse, when she arrived back to her own place, hot and flushed from their exhilarating 'champagne' celebration.

"Greetings, my little Haiwa!"

"Hi, Asad. Why do you call me 'little Eve'?"

"Because you remind me of Adam's spouse in the Koran! She was a Goddess, and so are you!"

"Then, if I am Eve, you must be Adam!"

"Ha-ha! V-ery good!"

"You're so conceited, Asad!"

"And you are so like your daughter with your quick words!"

"So, you've met her! She's arrived, already? Safely?"

"Safely, yes. But a little scared, a little shaken."

"And the other girl you've somehow acquired?"

"Very quiet. A dumb kitten among us tigers – yes?"

"You liken me to Eve and now you call me a tiger! Make up your mind, Asad!"

"You are my Eve, sweet-ling. I've rung to say I have again contacted your ex-husband, and he has agreed to pay my ransom price!"

"Really? How interesting... Paul must have acquired more capital! How soon can we celebrate again, when I can be forever with you?"

"I have given him time to collect his money together. Perhaps in a day or two, Little Haiwa. Be patient. In the meantime, your daughter stays in captivity. I shall enjoy her company!"

"Asad? You won't harm her?"

"Harm? No! No! Put any dark thoughts to the back of

your sharp mind, sweet-ling! But the other girl? Now, she could be a problem..."

"What would you do with her?"

"Perhaps arrange a little 'accident'? Or sell her on. I have plenty of contacts. Don't worry your head about it."

"Then I won't. Life will be sweet for us when Paul's money arrives!"

"Assuredly, little Haiwa, assuredly. Goodbye for now!"

As he replaced the elegant gold phone receiver back on its cradle, Asad was smiling, but it was a calculating, crooked smile.

# LONDON. INVOLVING POLICE

As soon as he agreed to the price, Paul called his friend, Ben Elliston.

"I've accepted the ransom price." There was a slight relief in his voice now that he felt he was doing something useful.

"How much do they want?"

"A certain amount. I can't tell you at the moment."

"Listen, Paul? I went to the club today and John Denby was there. You know he's a DCI on our patch? I nearly told him about you!"

"Don't say a thing, please Ben!"

"I didn't. But I think he could help if your in a jam! He's the strong, silent type – a bit like that bloke you hired!"

"No police. Silverman was emphatic on that!"

"I know. But if anything should go wrong? Well, I think I'd like the police to be around, wouldn't you?"

"Yes, but –"

"Paul? I think you should phone John and have a quiet word with him."

"I don't want to put Leigh in any danger!"

"You won't; the police would handle this properly, and they'd keep you informed!"

"No, Ben. I really can't. I'm frightened if they found out, what would they do to Leigh?"

Ben didn't reply. Paul pressed on. "I know you mean well, but I'll keep it quiet 'till I hear from Silverman. If he hasn't made any headway, I'll call John, right?"

"Okay, if you say so, although it goes against my better principles. The police have got the contacts and the know-how for this type of job, Paul. They've got certain departments that deal with things like this. I'll be thinking of you! Call you later, yeah?"

"Yeah, thanks, Ben. Bye."

After he rang off on his mobile, Ben pondered Paul's

predicament. "I don't suppose it would do any harm to tell John," he thought. He found himself looking up John's number on his mobile.

A firm, gruff voice answered Ben's call. "DCI Denby here? Oh, hello Ben, how are things with you?"

"I'm fine, but you know my near neighbor, Paul Wright?

"Paul Wright, the banker? Yeah?"

That's the man! Well, his daughter's been kidnapped!"

"You don't say! When was this? Has he reported it?"

"No. He doesn't want to endanger his daughter."

"What with police cuts and everything, I can't really help you, unless he reports the incident. But tell me what you know."

Ben recited to John all that Paul had told him. "You say the kidnappers have hold of two girls? Listen, Ben, I'll go and check our records, if someone's been in to report their daughter missing, I can act accordingly. It all happened at a nightclub called 'Minks' you say? All right. I'll see what I can do. Thanks for calling – bye!"

Thinking about this latest news an intrigued John Denby paid a visit to his division's main inquiry desk. He asked the sergeant there if anyone had reported a kidnapping, but he drew a blank, as he suspected he would.

He decided to go and report the incident to his superior, namely because he believed something could come of this.

His superior, when he heard the story, looked resigned. "Tales in the fog, John. This is probably a job for the special ops people. I don't think its our problem. But keep me informed if you hear anything. I know the night club you're talking of – my daughter goes there. There's no point in you seeing the place, it won't be open, 'cept to the cleaners. Chew on it, but we'll take no action as yet, although it's on our patch, right?"

"Right, sir." A resigned John left to get back to his office, and the matter was put to rest for the time being.

# ABU DHABI. IN THE DESERT

Rachid's 'old jalopy' took him, Karl, and their distinguished war guest, Dickie, to their desert destination, a large Bedouin camp roughly about 40 kilometers east of Abu Dhabi, out towards the small village of Al Wathba, which was enclosed by the desert. They started off on the E22 highway, knowing it would be a good half-hours drive, depending on how fast Rachid's shaky old car could go!

On the way, once out of Abu Dhabi's island traffic, now skirting the wind-whipped desert, Karl asked Rachid about any facts he'd found out about Farid Al Ghazzawi. He knew Rachid had an unfettered encyclopedic mind, and would feed him with the right information. The misshapen Arab might be work-wary and lazy, but was good on collecting interesting tit-bits of information.

Rachid, pleased to be asked, embarked on his facts with gusto. "He is one of the old-style Bedu's. He believes in being a good host – even to his enemies, and his hospitality, which we Arabs call Diyafa, is famous! His feasts are magnanimous and legendary. Like all Bedu's he loves his freedom, and he loves Allah! He is greathearted, calm and patient. His people think the world of him."

"He deals with oil, doesn't he?"

"He has made much profit from it. A lot of Arabs have! Many are billionaire's living in Abu Dhabi right now! Al Ghazzawi started in the oil fields as a young man, and he worked his way up, later commuting from his Bedu camp to the city. Even when the wells run dry he'll be comfortably off. Nowadays, he's rich enough to own several battery-operated satellite TV's, a car phone and several 4X4's. He also has the empathy and patience to train Peregrine Falcons, it's a Bedu thing! Although this sport has now become a status symbol for rich Arabs, who spend a fortune on obtaining their application fees, licenses, administration fees, and examination fee to own one of these rapturous birds! His hundred-strong people are probably the last nomads to keep wandering the deserts of the UAE! Other Bedu's have given up! But he still rides nearly everywhere on his beloved camels, following the big cars and vans across the country, carrying his tribe to far places!"

"I'm getting the picture. What about you, Dickie?"

"This Al Ghazzawi seems to be a resourceful man!"

Karl nodded. "I think he will be a very useful man. I'm looking forward to meeting him!"

When they arrived at the camp it was full of hustle and bustle. Women in red thobes and scarf-type headdresses were cooking something that smelled rich and appetizing over a cavernous fire. Younger women in blue robes carried plastic pitchers of water from a nearby water truck which had just arrived on the busy scene.

There were a range of black tents pitched, and it was a wonder how they stayed up against the vigorous north-westerly desert wind, so strong, it could have been a shamal, that constantly buffeted them. All the tents were held up with poles and fastened down with strong guy ropes very firmly driven into the sand.

A small string of heavily loaded camels, seen upon the far horizon, were plodding behind each other, returning home to the camp, eager for food and rest after a long morning's work. Some, their groaning, grunting bellowing could be heard across the expanse of yellow sand. Goats on leads were following the camels and their handlers, who were wearing black turbans against the heat of the sun.

Rachid noticed Karl's keen gaze and said:"The camels probably have food supplies for the camp. Even Bedu's have to buy frozen and processed goods from shops now! Times have changed! The camels are not used so much these days, by some Bedu's, but Al Ghazzawi still keeps his to ride on, and breeds them, mainly for camel racing, as

I've said! I believe they race special thoroughbred camels with radio-controlled mikes attached to their harness, and they chase them in fast cars to find out who wins! Near here is a camel-racing track which is as popular as our horse racing! It's very costly to own thoroughbred camels now! They also have quad bikes that they race in the desert, as well. Some Bedu's even practice para-gliding too."

"Did you say bikes?" Asked Derrick eagerly. He had misheard; he was thinking of his own ancient old motorbike tucked away, rusting at home in a shed, never to be used again.

"Rachid said quad bikes, they're more chunky and chubbier than the two-wheeler you had in your day!" Karl whispered to him in an aside, as they carefully helped the older man from the car.

"I remember my first second-hand motorbike only cost me ten shillings!" Derrick whispered back.

Karl laughed. "Was that in the war days, my friend?"

"Near enough! Don't forget, we were rationed then!"

They could see an Arabian fox loitering in the vicinity, cunningly awaiting an opportunity to steal food from the camp fire. He was partly hidden among a cone-shaped sand dune and had large ears and a small body. Enticed by the savory smell of the meat being cooked, he was out of his den early, ready to forage for his dinner.

Near one black tent, tethered by a short leash, perched outside enjoying the sun, wearing a dark hood, and sitting calmly on its weathering yard, facing the wind to feel safe, clung a patient-looking Peregrine Falcon! From what Karl could see of it's body, it was dark gray, it's underparts a pale white. It didn't seem at all shaken by the comings and goings of the camp!

Karl said to Rachid: "That Falcon looks serene and unruffled; it must have been fed recently!"

Rachid noticed his interest and whispered: "That wonderful creature has magnificent yellow eyes, and a black head! If it turned on you, it could tear your flesh apart with its hooked beak, causing terrible scars! It's a wild bird after all! Al Ghazzawi showed it to me earlier... Yes, it has fed! I have seen it perform – so swift, so fast, so high, its magnificent gliding wings takes your breath away! Arab's say working with a falcon is priceless. It's a great sport."

"I'll bet! Let's hope it doesn't bite! I don't fancy being torn apart by that arrogant sharp beak!"

It was to the largest black tent that Rachid led Karl and Derrick. As they entered, Karl noticed the air moved inside from open vents to give light and coolness to the interior. The desert was baking hot and he was glad he'd changed into his shorts and bought his navy blue cap!

And there, sitting grandly upon a throne of colorful linen cushions was Farid Al Ghazzawi, a stout little gnome with a pointed, short gray beard, hawk nose and bright, shrewd, wrinkled brown eyes, his rugged face and hands the color of old leather. Over his head and swathed around his neck was a plain black keffiyya, and over his dark thobe he wore a khaki colored aba, a kind of wide waistcoat. Loosely tied around his ample waist was a red tasseled sash.

The whole tent was filled with embroidered carpets and there were several men seated on the gaily colored rugs. Around the old Bedouin were four elder men, all wearing loose dark clothes and black keffiyya's, which absorbed the sun's harmful rays and protected them from the desert sand and the dry baking heat.

Four younger men, also wearing black head-cloths who looked like guards, came towards Karl. They had long, cruel-looking swords in their belts, which added to the mystic splendor of this Arabian knight's adventure, to Derrick's delight.

Al Ghazzawi spoke before his men reached them. His English was excellent.

"Let our guests come to me, but retrieve any weapons!"

Karl found his gun, the Ruger, lifted carefully from his pocket. He didn't resist, but bowed to the man who sat on his cushions like a prince.

"Greetings. I come in friendship. We seek your help on a matter that my friend Rachid, here, has already spoken to you about."

Al Ghazzawi rose from his seat in a fairly fluid fashion for such a rotund man. He advanced to Karl and rubbed his nose against Karl's. Then he did the same to Rachid and Derrick.

"Greetings, friends. Welcome to my windswept camp!"

He nodded to his elders and guards and casually waved them away. They all left, reluctantly.

He re-seated himself and waved to Karl and the other two men to do the same. The older women of the camp then entered and put down higher cushions for Derrick, assisting him to sit in such a way that squatting down to carpet level wasn't too uncomfortable for him. He didn't even need to use his stick.

Al Ghazzawi spoke to Derrick politely. "Now, tell me, you are comfortable, I hope?"

"I am fine, thank you. You have a wonderful, busy camp here!"

Al Ghazzawi looked pleased. "It is my Bedu kingdom – like your home is your kingdom!"

"If you put it like that, I suppose it is! You speak English so well!"

"I have been taught by my family. All my children have gone to Universities here. Despite being a Bedu I was lucky enough to gain citizenship status in 1992, through my long friendship with an oil baron back when we first imported crude oil in early 1962! He had friends in high places who cast a blind eye upon our lack of illiteracy and our unreliable source of living, but took our earnings which we had accrued from oil! Being rich enabled me to send my children to university at last! In the early days they lacked proper schooling, and did not speak English. We were bidoun, and schools did not then accept children without papers or passport!"

"I didn't realize... That's tough! How many children do

you have?"

"Hah! They have grown now. I have a daughter and three sons, the youngest is away at University, studying, but my second son is the black sheep of the family, if you see what I mean? Let me tell you something of him..."

"I am an old man now," Al Ghazzawi continued, speaking softly. "But in my youth I was fiery and strong! That was the time when we navigated by the sun and stars and slept beneath them on the sand! I had many caravan routes, which people paid us to travel on across the dessert, with goats and strings of gentle camels that carried our large loads! We'd average roughly about 40km in a day! Our deserts are large areas; they extend into portions of Iraq, southern Jordan, central Qatar, most of Abu Dhabi, western Oman, and north-eastern Yemen! I have been to all, between the spring hazes, a few torrential rains, and our 50 miles an hour dust storms which we call haboob! A haboob is a nightmare when it increases beyond it's strength! You cannot even see your hand in front of you!"

"I can imagine... It sounds fascinating! Are you what they call a pastoral Bedouin?"

"A warrior Bedu I prefer to call myself! I hail from Al-Ain, and was born into the Dhawahir tribe, but we had an uneasy relationship with the Na'im tribe, and we frequently fought disputes with each other! In my youth we would plan a ghazwas, attacking the Na'im for stealing our livestock from us!"

"What is a ghazwas?"

"It means a raid. Yes, we had plenty of those in the old days, when we paid homage to our sheikdoms and our wryly sheikhs, whose attacks on other tribes the British ignored! We were still under British protectorate in 1951, known as the Trucial States. Now, we have had 10,000 people arrive here since the 1960's. We finally gained UAE independence in 1971. I was fresh and eager then, for new experiences! And once, being young, I was indiscreet with a married woman! You understand me? It is against Sharia law! Our Penal Code disallows making love outside of marriage. It is haram, forbidden! It upsets the teachings of the Qur'an, that says we must worship only Allah! Neither must we drink intoxicants, it is khamr! A severe punishment follows if we're found out! But, enough of me, now, hear me tell you why I must kill my bastard son!"

Rachid gasped, and Derrick's mouth dropped open in surprise, but Karl remained unperturbed. He remembered how intent, fierce and fiery the Bedouin people were. The old-time Bedouin's used to have their own laws in the desert. He stayed motionless, listening with great interest.

"I let dear Fatima's husband, Mifsud Boulos, bring up the child, thinking him to be his, even though my heart cried to not have him here, with me, to bring up as a good Bedu boy."

"But I was proud of him then, (for I followed his affairs from a distance), when he went to the British University, so far away! When he came back, cultured but weak, I learned he had taken a great interest in the antiquities and artifacts of our country. He brought and sold and amassed much money, but he had become involved in darker things too."

"Now, he has everything he could ask for, including owning his own hotel, but money has gone to his head, he grabs it greedily! He is more in love with it than with life! More in love with himself than that woman who secretly calls herself his lover!"

"You mean Serena Wright?" Karl asked, quickly, as he listened intently to the old Bedouin's damning speech of his bastard son.

Karl noticed that Derrick shot him a quizzical glance when he mentioned Serena Wright's name, but the RAF man didn't say anything, keeping his surprise to himself. Derrick had obviously read the much-talked about break-up of Paul Wright's and Serena Wright's marriage, cited in the newspapers over two years back and echoed by the media all over the world.

There had followed an expensive divorce, resulting in a

wealthy Serena leaving Britain and settling in another country, surrounded by influential men-friends, some who had been boyfriends in her not-so-distant past... It was rumored she sometimes kept in touch with her estranged daughter and Paul Wright when she wanted money.

"The very woman! Please excuse my swearing. This is between us; no one else must hear me! A bitch on heat, that one! Sorry, it is forbidden for us to blaspheme in public! Since then I have carried out an exhaustive investigation into my sons life and found him wanting! He is an abomination to Arab society, and he has defaced what being a true Bedu is all about! So I am here, to pitch my camp and confront the evil man my son has become! To me, Asad is no longer Bedu! I am not afraid to denounce him, or own that I am his real father. I will take the consequences of this if it occurs, and the police find out! That is why I will help you in this dishonorable situation, Karl Silverman!"

Liking the forthright way Al Ghazzawi conducted his business, Karl straight away outlined his plans to this intelligent, talkative Bedouin.

Rachid listened, and Derrick, to his consternation, actually fell asleep on the fat, comfy cushions. He missed hearing what was planned.

The old Bedouin nodded his head when he'd heard Karl's strategy. "Yes, it is good! We can do this in the name of Allah! Your idea takes me back to when I was a young man, listening to my elders plots and plans!"

Derrick awoke with a start, hearing Karl say insistently: "But the timing must be perfect!"

"Of course. My men will be ready for our ghazwas! I will pick out the best for you! Now, Karl Silverman and friends, with our business over, let me share the hospitality of my tent with you!"

He clapped his hands like a lord, and the women of the camp entered again, coming out from behind a cloth curtain, where Karl assumed they had their quarters, bearing heavy trays of food and drink, which they deposited on their colorful handmade rugs and carpets.

Al Ghazzawi bent down and speared the side of a roasted sheep. The fat that spurted out, he captured with his finger and smeared it onto Karl's lips. He said: "It should be blood, not fat, but this is my way of welcoming you!" He then produced a small cup.

"Have some Kahwa. It is aromatic coffee made with cardamom powder, saffron, and rosewater. I shall pour it for you. It will be an honor."

Karl supped from the small cup. "Thank you. I like it!"

When he and the other two were offered roasted sheep in mounds of rice, with pine nuts, Karl remembered that Rachid had advised him, as a guest, not to eat with his left hand. To the Arabs this was considered unclean. He saw the whole dish was dressed in a rich white sauce made from yogurt and butter. It was followed by rice dates, fruit, and more yogurt.

Derrick found some of the food a little too rich for his liking, but he ate small portions of the warm, cooked meat with a little sauce, and he quite enjoyed the creamy yogurt!

Rachid said to Karl: "If you do not want any more coffee, shake the cup from side to side!"

Karl did so, and Al Ghazzawi's beautiful daughter, Leda, came out of the women's quarter and willingly, with a delighted smile, took it away. She was dressed in blue, the young girls color. Red, he learned, was for the married women. Leda was the same height as Karl, comely, with long braided locks that hung down either side of her face, escaping from her blue veiled coiled scarf she wore over her head. She glowed, her thin, high cheek-boned face delicately shaded by the natural cosmetics of the desert sun, and her hazel-looking wide eyes were etched in antimony, creating the exotic look of the eastern traveler against the desert's glare. All the men were taken with her beauty. Inimitably she was in a class of her own.

Leda seemed taken with Karl, Derrick noticed. She sat between Karl and Derrick, and constantly plied one or the other with little sweetmeats and delicacies.

She was also sweetly attentive to Derrick, and he basked in her friendly warmth like a sand lizard seeking the sun.

"Have another sweetmeat Derrick. There are plenty here!"

"Thank you, my dear, I'm full!" Refreshed and alert, he patted his stomach. He looked around him, at the colorful trappings of this busy Bedouin camp. He guessed it to be a hard life, yet the men and women seemed happy enough, and Leda appeared serene and thoughtful. He asked her:

"Have you always lived out here?"

"Oh, yes!" Her bright, hazel eyes shone softly over the dun-colored dunes lying in swirly ridges beyond the camp. "The desert has always been my home – apart from the time when I was at university, studying and learning about the world! But I'll always return to father's camp. I love this wandering life!"

"Yet you have such wonderful skin for one who lives out in the open!"

Leda blushed and laughed at the same time. She was aware Karl was listening to their conversation.

"Forgive me for being rude! I spoke out of turn!" Derrick spoke, shame-faced.

"Don't worry!" She soothed him in a dulcet tone, looking amused. "I understand your curiosity!" She bent to his ear, and whispered a few words in it.

Derrick's eyes widened. "Do you really?" He asked.

Karl said: "What's that? Do I get to hear?"

"No!" She said playfully. "I only tell Derrick the secrets of my beauty routine!"

Karl looked at her ruefully. "Why not tell me?"

Leda gave him a direct, cheeky answer: "Ah! Can you not tell that Derrick is my favorite!" She teased him, with a throaty laugh.

Karl shook his head, giving in, smiling broadly at her instant quip. He knew she was flirting with him as bait, and he gave in to her mischievous banter, enjoying her sunny, friendly warmth as Dickie was.

They'd eaten the meal with their fingers. Karl followed Rachid's example of rolling the rice into a ball and stuffing it into his mouth. Another male Bedouin who'd entered the tent for the feast, offered Karl his dagger to cut off a chunk of meat from the roasted sheep. Al Ghazzawi introduced him proudly to his guests, as his eldest son, Akmer. Akmer was tall and lean with youthful glowing brown skin the color of his father's. He wore desert attire like the other men of the tribe, and had a wolfish, but engaging smile.

Al Ghazzawi beamed happily at all the men seated around him, pleased they had eaten and enjoyed the rich meal. His charm and benevolent attitude towards his guests shone through like a ray of sunshine entering the huge tent. After waiting for his guests to finish, he then ate his helping of the food, it being polite for the host to eat last.

Karl was amazed at this sumptuous hospitality, but aware that time was ticking by. As soon as his host had finished, Karl asked him if he could pick out his men.

Al Ghazzawi said: "I have a camp of about a hundred people! I think 15 men will suffice for our little ghazwas!"

"They need to be sharp, but careful. What weapons do they have?"

Al Ghazzawi laughed. "We are not so back-of-the-beyond here! We have daggers and swords, and we have rifles. They should be adequate!"

"Rifles!"Derrick mused. "What do Bedouin's want with rifles! Are they licit?"

"Very!" Al Ghazzawi winked at Derrick. "By law, we do not use them often, the government only allow us a small ration of ammunition. We have licenses. The rifles are handy when food is scarce; like precious water found under dew-drenched rocks, it is our passport for survival in the desert! Without our water and food, whether it be processed or natural, we would die! By modern standards today, we have the water lorry visit us. As I said, we are not old-fashioned here! We are rich with life and love!"

Smiling agreement, Karl nodded, very taken himself by Al Ghazzawi's brisk and forthright manner.

When they left, the tribal leader gave them all a messy kiss on the lips. To the surprised Derrick, who had been helped to his feet by a few returning Bedouin women, he said stoutly: "This is our way of saying goodbye!"

He politely handed Karl back his gun, given to him by one of his men who had just entered the broad tent. "I'll await your return, my friend. Our women will be ready for you!"

# ABU DHABI. HOMESICK

After speaking chokingly to her father, Leigh felt very upset. She was taken back to her room, shaken and dejected. When she saw Leigh's tears Fran forgot her own worries and put her arms around the taller girl.

Leigh said bitterly: "Oh boy, but did I totally lose it! I'm burnt!"

"It's okay to cry, Leigh, your father knows now. Something will be done."

"I bloody hope so! This horrible heat is driving me crazy! It's so hot and airless!"

"There's a fan going over there. Sit by it, and cool down a bit."

Leigh grabbed hold of her friend's hand.

"Thanks for being here for me!"

Awkwardly, Fran replied: "That's okay. It's my own fault I got in the way – too impulsive!"

"Were you always impulsive?"

"Not really. It was just seeing you tied up, it alarmed me, and I didn't like the way that boy claimed they were your friends. I thought you'd come on your own? I didn't trust him – his explanation stank!"

"I don't remember them much. Only the girl with plaited hair."

"I remember the boy's heavy glasses. I think they were hired to do the dirty work for those Arab men!"

"S'pect you're right – you've obviously worked it out! What a cheek that Boulos thug has, dragging us here like this!"

"Yes." Fran looked worried. "He's arranged this whole monstrous thing! I don't like the sound of it!"

"Me, neither. He's a creep!"

Fran nodded uneasily. She changed the subject by asking Leigh: "Was it wise to go to 'Minks' on your own, after that first kidnap attempt?"

"Not really, no. Pretty dumb, huh? But I'd got over what happened in June. Last night, I met up with some friends, and asked them to come clubbing with me, but they didn't want to! They were snobs, preferring to dress up for an upper-class fund-raising Gala, which is so boring and dull! I decided to shoot off to 'Minks' alone! I sloshed Coco Mademoiselle over me, changed into my gold dress, and took off! I'm sure that gang followed me to 'Minks'. They must have been watching out for me!"

"Yeah, they knew where you were all right!"

"I've often dared myself to go to 'Minks' on my own. It's so much freer than an expensive Debutante's Ball or a prim old cocktail party! You never know who you are going to meet at 'Minks'! But I should have been more careful after that first kidnap attempt! I didn't dream I might be followed! I think I saw you come through the doors after I arrived?"

"That's right. I went straight to the bar to tank myself up!"

"Why did you want to get drunk?"

"Oh, boyfriend trouble, you know!"

"He let you down?"

"Er, something like that! How about you? Have you got a boyfriend?"

"Not at the moment. But I did fancy that man who was dancing with us! Some mover!"

Both girls smiled over the memory, then sobered as they remembered their predicament.

"I hope daddy pays that sod soon! I hate being locked in! We must have slept for hours, only to find ourselves prisoners in this mad Ali-Barber land! I still can't take it in!"

"Yeah, it's so unreal! Maybe we should rest up a bit? The injection they stabbed us with is still making me feel sleepy! We need to keep our strength up, Leigh. A good rest will help us cool down a little."

"You sound a bit of a wise owl. How old are you?"

"Er, eighteen!"

"I'm seventeen, but because I'm tall I can get away with looking older!"

"Do debutante's and socialite's work?" Fran asked casually, as the restless Leigh flopped onto her bed.

Leigh made a face. "I helped in the office, on my dad's estate. But I wasn't properly paid for it! Daddy gives me some money every week, and I spend it! That's my life, really – wasted! What about you?"

"Oh, I have a paid job decorating front windows for a posh up-market charity shop!"

"A charity shop? Wow! Is it interesting?"

"The customers are; they bring in fantastic items to sell!"

"When daddy's paid for me, and I'm free, I might ask him if I can go work in a charity shop! It sounds fun! Whatever is the matter, Fran – you're face has dropped!"

Fran sighed. "I'm just wondering who is going to pay for me? My parent's aren't rich!"

"I hadn't thought of that! Whatever will that cheat do with you? I can't let him send you to a sex shop! Oh, I can't have this! Daddy will have to pay!"

"Oh, Leigh!"

"Well, I can't leave you here! Not with that beast!"

The two girls hugged each other. Fran looked happier. "Right, I'm going to sleep this heavy meal off!" She decided practically.

Leigh sighed. "Might as well, there isn't much to do except look at the funny clothes in the wardrobe. There's no magazines in here, and I'm bored! I'll follow your example and hope the time goes quick." Leigh peeled off her false eyelashes as she spoke. Her eyes looked bare, somehow larger without them. She looked at her white, square, perspiring face in the mirror and sighed: "Wish I could put the clock back. I want to get home – badly!"

# ABU DHABI. RAGE

"Asad! Asad! You prick!" Serena Wright was beside herself with anger. "What do you mean by ordering your thugs to my apartment, in broad daylight, with their guns on show, threatening me, like I'm some mobster's doll! What are you thinking of?"

"I am thinking my dearest one, that it would be good to give your daughter a surprise!"

"Surprise – what surprise?"

"You, of course!"

"Me? How do you mean?"

"You are to be put in with the girls at gunpoint to show your daughter your love for her!"

"But, Asad, I can't! She mustn't know –!"

"That you are co-scheming with me? Life would be so bitter-sweet for your both, don't you think?"

"You bastard! Asad, what have I –?"

"Nothing, sweet-ling. It is part of my plan! You will do this, or my men will kill you! It's as simple as that!"

"You have never spoken to me like this before, you two-timing sod!"

"Perhaps my true heart lies unveiled now."

"You were using me!"

"That is so, I can admit this now!"

"Here I am, living like a pauper in Abu Dhabi, hoping to become a citizen through marriage to you, and you're letting me down, really Big Time! Why do you think I stay in my flat here, separate from you? So our lusty union isn't discovered by the government, or police! I could tell them about you and your schemes, they'd investigate and you'd be punished!"

"Dearest Serena, don't speak to me like that! My men

have guns – remember – and they will use them! Do you really want to be killed for telling tales against me? Equally, if you did admit our clandestine union, you would be flogged and interned, or deported to some terrible prison camp in Yemen! Think about it!"

"Asad! You're breaking my heart! Show some mercy, please!"

All he said was, coldly: "I shall expect you soon." Leaving Serena to screech at the ceiling and all but tear her hair out at Asad's duplicity.

What a fool she'd been! She had nothing to fight back with, and Emir and Ameen were waiting for her outside. There seemed no escape; for once in her life she was frightened of what she'd risked in Asad's favour, thinking he loved her, and allowing herself to be drawn into his web of deceit and crooked schemes...

There were tears of pained disillusion in her eyes as she left her apartment for the last time, hedged in by Asad's brutal, watchful Arabs, their guns hidden behind her back, edging her unceremoniously towards their parked car as quickly as they dared.

# LONDON. SOUNDING THE ALARM

Kostas had opened his coffee shop that Saturday morning and waited, expectantly, for Tanja to turn up. He was looking forward to seeing her and her daughter again. When she didn't appear, he began to worry. She was usually on time. Her apartment was very close to his shop. Perhaps the child was ill? He was puzzled she hadn't phoned him to say so. On impulse, as he wasn't busy yet, he shut up shop and walked quickly to her apartment, still wearing his serving apron, to find out for himself what was happening.

To his horror and confusion he found the apartment door lock had been forcefully split open, and when he looked inside, he could find no trace of Tanja and Kimmi!

Panicking, fearing all sorts of bad things, Kostas phoned the police. He waited for them to arrive and search the apartment. They questioned the distraught Kostas, and hunted around the apartment for clues. Kostas knew enough to tell them about Tanja's friend, Karl, who had obtained this place for her. Then they found a phone book in Tanja's bedside drawer with Karl's home and work's phone numbers in. There was no answer at Karl's private address, and they didn't bother to leave a message on his answer-phone, so they contacted his works 'department' number. A female voice answered: "CIUSO? How can I help you?"

The police officer looked astonished. He had heard of the mysterious CIUSO – they were an elite branch of the police force! He said, hesitantly: "I'm a police constable, based in Peckham, London. I want to speak to Mr Karl Silverman. Is he there?"

"I'm not allowed to say... He may be away at present. Is

it urgent? Perhaps you'd like to speak to the Commander-in-Chief?"

"Yes, it is! I'd like to speak to someone! I'm making an important routine inquiry that may involve Mr Silverman!"

"I'll get the Commander-in-Chief for you. Hold on, please."

A man came on the line with a blunt, austere voice: "Yes? What does a police constable want with Silverman?"

The policeman explained his urgent call. The man with the blunt, austere voice became sharp and concise, he ordered: "Step down from this incident, constable, and don't report it to your superiors! Were you called out to give assistance?"

"Er, yes sir!"

"Then give me your name and number! And that of your colleague if you have one! I'll have a word with your superior where you are based, and get him to strike off your attendance-to-crime-scene from the duty rota!"

"You mean – me and partner are off the case?"

"That's right!"

"But sir, I can't leave the occupier's flat unattended! The front door's without a lock!"

"You have my full authority to step down! My people will take it from here and continue the investigation as from now! The case is closed to you and your colleague! Understood?"

"Ye-es, sir, but what about the shop owner who came round and found the place empty? He's still here with us."

"Tell him to go home and continue his work."

"Sir, he's very worried..."

"He works nearby, at a coffee-shop you say?"

"Yes."

"Inform him that my men will have a word with him later. Impress on him he must say nothing of what has happened. We'll take care of everything – including the lock on the front door! Goodbye!"

# LONDON. CONCERNS

"It's afternoon now, Nigel. Something must have happened to Fran – she'd never go this long without phoning me!" Exclaimed Mandy Tompkins, worriedly.

"Well, what do you want me to do?"

"I want us to go to charity shop that Fran works at, maybe their short-staffed or something, and needed her to come in to help out?"

"If it puts your mind at rest dear...okay, I'll get the car out!"

Driving to the charity shop called Daisies, Nigel said: "Surely the shop didn't call her back in to work late last night? Charity shops don't have those sort of hours!"

"I'm sure I don't know! It is a posh place she works at! No, she must have gone out somewhere, and something has happened to her!"

They soon arrived outside Daisies, and managed to squeeze into a space outside the shop door, that was on a line. "I can't stop long, love, there could be a hidden camera around, taking a picture of us for all I know! I don't want to get a fine!"

"Drive round the block a few times. I'll get out and take a quick look inside. Won't be long!"

As she got out, Mandy noticed a few clothes bags piled up in the shop's doorway, but it appeared to be shut! "Odd, for a busy Saturday!" Mandy mused. Then she saw a large white notice stuck on the door.

She went back to find their car, frowning, which Nigel had parked legally, further down the road. "I don't get it, Nigel. The shop's shut down. It's been closed since 2016!"

Nigel listened to her news and looked worried. "If it's been shut for over a year, where the hell has Fran been working all this time?"

"I don't know, but we could drive to the address written on the door. Maybe Fran forgot to tell me she'd moved shops?"

They drove on to the new address, which was open, but the shop manageress did not know any Fran Tompkins! Was Fran a voluntary worker, the lady asked?

"No. She was doing a paid job!" Mandy answered her.

Nigel and Mandy were mystified.

"Where can she be?"

Nigel had an idea. "Let's drive to her flat. Perhaps she's come back?"

They drove to Fran's address and rang the doorbell. A very sleepy female voice called out: "Who is it?"

"Mr and Mrs Tompkins." Nigel called back. "Is Fran there yet?"

The door was unlocked and opened to reveal a surprised Isabelle in a white, lacy dressing gown. "You've woken me up!" She mumbled, bemused.

"We're sorry, Isabelle, but Fran's still not turned up, and we're worried about her. We had to find out if she'd come back here?" Mandy asked.

"No, she hasn't. I honestly haven't seen anything of her since early last night!"

"Did she say where she was going off to?" Asked Nigel.

"No, sorry. She sometimes leaves me a note, but there isn't one here – you're welcome to look!"

All three searched for any note Fran may have left; they found nothing.

"That settles it, Nigel, I think we should call the police!" Mandy decided.

"I think you have to wait a few more hours 'till they'll let you make a claim!" Exclaimed Isabelle.

"Oh, dear! Fran, where are you?" Her mother moaned, wringing her hands.

# ABU DHABI.
# NEWS AT THE FORCE'S HOTEL

Rachid drove Karl and Derrick back to their hotel and left them there. Karl had not outlined all his plans to the ex-squadron leader, but they had arranged to meet each other later, as Dickie requested to return with Karl to the Bedouin camp. Karl had asked Rachid if he'd pick up Derrick later that night, at a specific, arranged time, which the slouchy, humped Arab promised to do – for extra cash!

Derrick had expressed a wish 'to be part of the scene'. Karl had made one stipulation: Dickie was to stay in the Bedouin camp and not take part in the raid. Karl didn't want anyone else endangered, in case the ghazwas got out of hand!

Derrick heartily agreed, saying: "What ghazwas? But you're right not to involve me. I'll leave the action to you youngsters!"

In front of Derrick, Karl made some important calls to England, then he phoned Paul Wright.

"Are you going to pay the ransom when they ask for it?"

"Yes, I want my daughter back, as soon as you can! She must be so frightened stuck out there!"

"I understand. I'm working on it. Trust me!"

"You keep saying that! But I had Ben Elliston on the phone again. He wants me –"

"I know, he wants you to call the police, (and it makes me wonder why)! Believe me, it isn't good to involve the police at the moment!"

"Ben is a friend, and you wonder why he wants to help me? Jesus God, man! My daughter's life –!"

"I have a plan to get her home to you, so long as you do what I ask, and leave the police out of it!"

"You're really asking a lot, Silverman!"

"I still need your co-operation. I will not let Leigh, or the other girl get hurt, if I can help it! Have you rested?"

"Not yet. I've gone past sleep... I don't think I can, even if I wanted to!"

"You must rest. You'll be surprised how much it will help you. Take a sleeping pill if you have any, and leave the worrying to me!"

"I can't switch off; something might happen..."

Karl sighed. "And it might not. Do what you think best. I must go now. Goodbye."

To Derrick, he said: "The father can't trust me; he's already spoken to someone else re his daughter's kidnap."

"That's because you're so secretive, Karl. You trust me, yet you still haven't told me all!"

"Not yet, no. Young lives are at stake and I don't want this to go wrong! My plan might not end up as I hope! Someone could die, and it would be my responsibility if they do!"

"Don't be hard on yourself! You're used to death, Karl!"

"But not the death of others, if I can help it! I face this every time I'm on a mission: death doesn't scare me. I've made my peace with it, but it's scary for others. I'm aware, introspectively, that I could easily lead these girls into danger with my unorthodox plan, even with CIUSO's backing! Like I've probably placed Tanja and Kimmi in danger through my thoughtless act of settling them in Britain!"

"You undermine yourself. It wasn't 'thoughtless' of you to try and assist them! You say this woman asked you to help her?"

"Yes! She was in a dead-end place. She pleaded for help!"

"You have that kind of 'man-of-the-world' face, Karl. Women, especially, are drawn to trust you, somehow sensing you won't let them down! You did what you thought was right – which is so like you!"

"It's got me in an awkward spot! I'm swearing at myself over Tanja and Kimmi's demise! I realize how Paul Wright feels about his daughter now!"

"It's tough, I know, but stick it out! I'm sure you're plans are sound. I believe in you!"

"Thanks, Dickie."

"I have to ask, Karl, it's funny... I've never known your family situation! Have you any?"

"No, I'm an orphan. Like the woman I told you about. I kidded myself I was helping her out, but she had different ideas about me! As for my plans tonight, I place my trust in divine intervention!"

"You speak like a man who's found God!"

Karl raised an eyebrow. "Maybe I have!" He said, bemusedly. "All I know is, if I die tonight, I will have done my best. That's good enough for me!"

"For any man." Derrick murmured. "Tell me a little more about Paul Wright's associates? I sense you're holding something back!"

Later, both Karl and Derrick withdrew to their rooms to have a short rest. Karl showered quickly, using cold water, and changed back into his bootleg jeans, then relaxed, fully clothed on his large bed, sorting through his mobile and answering any messages left on it. He was glad to notice that 'the den' had been busy on his behalf. They'd messaged him to tell him they'd found the stolen getaway car that Tanja and Kimmi had been taken away in. An attempt had been made to fire the car, but had not succeeded because of a passing farmer in his tractor, who noticed two men acting suspiciously in woodland on his property. His curious approach had deterred the men. Some CIUSO operatives were now busy tracking the men down, getting descriptions of them from the farmer. The good news brightened his mood.

He also learned that Derrick's son had contacted Dickie on the hotel switchboard. Dickie's in-laws wouldn't be back until late. He'd already told his son not to worry about him; he would be out with a friend, and his son and wife didn't have to stay up for him, unless they wanted to!

Having perused all this information to his satisfaction, Karl set his mobile's alarm again, still wondering how Tanja and Kimmi were faring, and managed a troubled catnap.

# ABU DHABI. A SURPRISE!

Shaken to the core, Serena followed Asad's men, who lead her by gunpoint to the bedroom where the girls were locked in.

She stopped, just outside the ornately-carved wooden door, and pleaded with a whispered: "Please, can I go to another room?"

Emir spoke as softly as she: "It is not permitted."

Serena looked desperate at his answer. She tried saying: "But I'm still Asad's favorite woman, really, I am! He's a devil, he's just play-acting with us! Pulling our legs!"

Emir momentarily looked confused, not understanding her English expression. "Madam, it is ordered, you must go in with the girls! NOW, go in! No more arguments!"

"Look, I can pay you both double what he does, if you want to come and work for me?"

"I work only for my master, as does Ameen! We do not take foreigner's bribes, you stupid female!"

"Don't call me names! You both know me by now? I'm Asad's mistress for God's sake!"

"Quiet!" The gun was being rammed into her back again, and she was forced, with great reluctance, to walk towards the door, one slow step at a time, feeling desperate and sensing disaster looming.

"Oh, Christ, you bloody ignorant peasants! Put me somewhere else – anywhere but in there with them!"

"It is ordered. I obey only my master!" Emir unlocked the door as he spoke, pushing a sullen, obstinate Serena inside, re-locking the door quickly, before she could react.

"Sods!" Serena whispered under her breath, aware her heart was racing with tension.

The room was in semi-darkness, the fan still whirring

away. Both girls were lying drowsily on their beds wearing their hated Arab attire. When they heard the door being unlocked again, they sat up, alerted, two dim silhouette's in a shaded room, their minds asking what was happening now? Both were terrified of their situation, facing the unknown anxiously with quickening heartbeats.

Serena put on a brave front, squaring her shoulders.

"Darling! Guess who's here?"

"Mother? Is that you?" Called Leigh's disbelieving voice from out of the shadows.

"Yes, darling, it's me!"

"I don't believe this – mother? I never thought to hear your voice in this godforsaken place! How come you're here?" Leigh sounded exhausted and puzzled.

"I've been taken, like you two!"

Out of the dimness, Fran's voice asked, also puzzled: "Leigh, you're mother's here? I don't understand?"

"Are you all right, daughter?" The words sounded stiff coming from Serena's lips.

Leigh, halfheartedly tried to answer her mother, as she leaned over to snap on the crystal lamp that lay on a small ebony table between the two beds. "I suppose so... If you must know, it's been real scary and strange! How come they got you?"

"Oh, I was in the wrong place at the wrong time!"

Leigh echoed Fran's words. "I don't understand, why you, though? Surely daddy hasn't got to pay for you as well as me? What a swine that Boulos thug is! Do you know, you've only called me twice in the past two years? Where have you been?"

"Oh, traveling here and there! I've settled now, got an apartment in Abu Dhabi."

"Here!"

"Yes, a modern apartment in the city."

"Huh, well daddy gave you enough money towards your divorce deal for you to buy a mansion with it! I bet you're with a man! Anybody I know?" Suspicion of her mother's past antics had sharpened Leigh's voice.

"No, dear, I'm with nobody."

"That's unusual. You're always with a man!"

"My sex life is not your concern, Leigh –"

Serena broke off as the door opened. Emir came in bringing them sweet tea. Serena had hoped to spot Asad with them, but the greedy Arab wasn't around, to the woman's disappointment. She wanted to confront him, plead her love towards him. She'd swallowed her bitter pride over his sudden, disarming treatment of her. Such were the stakes, she was prepared to beg for leniency again, realizing what a jam she was in without his protective backing...

Emir quietly left the tea on a larger ebony table, and left swiftly, locking the door after him.

"God! I'm thirsty!" Leigh swooped on the tea and gulped it down. She made a face and spat the mouthful out. "This tea's disgusting – it's too sweet!"

"Drink it slowly." Fran advised.

Serena turned to her, as if noticing Fran for the first time. "Who are you?"

"My friend." Leigh spoke quickly. "She got taken along with me!"

"And what is your name?" Queried Serena smoothly, sounding like some demanding royal monarch.

"It's Fran." Said Fran, not liking the woman much. In the lit-up room she could see that Serena had a model figure and a model's made-up face. Her hard cheekbones were accentuated by cunning, expensive cosmetics, and her curly hair was bleached golden blond. She smelt of a strong, musky perfume, and had tapered red fingernails and red lipstick plastered on thin lips. Despite her assured, modeled guise, her make-up looked old-fashioned and heavy. Fran thought Leigh must take after her father; Serena's regal face was not so square as her daughter's.

"Pleased to meet you, Fran. It seams we're all in the same boat!"

Fran nodded, but she didn't take Serena's proffered hand. Instead, she heard herself say:

"You haven't said a proper hello to your daughter yet. Fran needs your love. She's lonely!"

"My dear, how remiss of me, come here Leigh!"

As Leigh ran to her with a sob, Serena looked over her daughter's shoulder at Fran, who was shocked to notice no smile of maternal welcome on Serena's fixed face.

It made Fran glad that her family loved her. This woman was a cold bitch! Fran pushed down the wave of homesickness she felt when she thought of her parents, and tried to feel happy for Leigh having her mother here to vent her tears on. But Serena's lukewarm, feeble greeting didn't seem right somehow, and Leigh had acted suspicious and wary of her mother's surprise arrival; Fran sensed some sort of unspoken tension or jealousy between the pair of them.

She wondered if Serena's sudden intrusion would help or hinder their predicament...

# SATURDAY. ESCAPE HOPE!

Someone had come back! Tanja heard the front door being opened. She had no idea of the time. The little box room they were in had no window, only the one naked light bulb hanging from the ceiling, so she didn't know whether it was night or day!

She and Kimmi were hungry. They had eaten nothing since they'd been abducted, and it seemed like they'd been stuck in this room for hours!

She grabbed Kimmi to her, wishing there was something in the room that she could use against their abductors. She'd thrash the living daylights out of them, keeping them penned in here like cattle!

She heard someone laugh, two men were talking to each other. After about five minutes, she heard footsteps on lino coming towards their locked room.

A throaty, Kent accent called out: "Move away from the door! No tricks, now – I'm coming in!"

"Mummy!" Kimmi clung to her, frightened again.

"Shhh! Shhh, darling! It's all right!"

The same burly man who had picked Kimmi up, came in, opening the door wide for his companion, who bore a tin tray in his hands with some kind of steaming-hot meal on it.

At last, it looked like they were being fed!

The man with the tray deposited their meal on the dusty floor. Tanja flared up: "Are we supposed to eat like dogs! We need chairs!"

The man pointed to his companion. "He's going to bring some in! Satisfied?"

The aroma of hot food was tantalizing! Mother and daughter waited, fidgeting, for the chairs to be brought in. When the men left, locking the door, they both fell on the ready-made microwave meals in individual trays, and began to eat with their plastic forks hungrily.

It was some kind of Paella dish with very few prawns and loads of saffron colored rice. Kimmi ate all hers without complaining that the prawns were too chewy. Tanja did the same. Replete, they sat back in their hard, wooden kitchen chairs and tried to relax.

Tanja's mind raced; the chairs they were sitting on were the only heavy things in this room! These foolish men had not seemed to realize they had given her something she could use as a weapon! Did she have the strength to wield it, she wondered? She stood up and lifted the chair, holding it with two hands held opposite each side of the seat, so that the legs of the chair were raised like four prongs in front of her. It was heavy. She couldn't hold it for long without her shoulders aching.

"What are you doing, mummy?"

"Trying something, darling. Stay near me when the men come back for the chairs. We might be able to get out!"

# ABU DHABI, INTRUSION

Men dressed all in black stealthily entered Karl's hotel apartment in the evening, just after 6.30 UAE standard time, before his alarm went off.

They gathered around his bed as he lay sleeping, all holding hunting rifles, and they looked dangerous!

He awoke by some sixth sense of danger, seeing the five men in his room, and instantly reached for his Ruger as it nestled under his pillow; it was the second one he'd obtained discreetly from the middle-eastern ex-pat agent.

But the gun wasn't there!

He swung his body out of bed preparing to fight.

His gun was held in the firm hand of the man who faced him, and that man was grinning wickedly.

Karl gave in. He said defeatedly, "Okay Akmer, you win! You said you'd get in somehow, and you did – all five of you! That takes some doing!"

The man he spoke to chuckled. "Yes, it is I. Are you pleased with my boast that we'd enter like shadows in the night and you wouldn't hear us? We are stealthy warriors at heart, and we look forward to doing this again, later. But for now, it is time to go!"

He gave Karl one of his wolfish smiles, his eyes dark and lively, relishing this adventure. His jet-black goatee beard and narrow aesthetic face seemed to shimmer in the shaded light of the air-conditioned hotel room. He was like a sea captain, a pirate of old, expectantly and excitedly awaiting the unknown.

Karl, keyed up himself, caught the other man's buoyant mood. He replied firmly as he slipped on his clothes. "I'm ready Akmer. I hope your father is waiting for me back at the camp!"

"He is ready. Everything you asked for has been arranged. The women are ready for you also. They have prepared an experience you will not forget!"

"God save the women!" Karl gave a heart-felt whistle. "It all sounds good!"

He called Derrick on his mobile and told the sleepy voice at the other end: "I'm leaving soon, if you still want to come with me, Dickie?"

With a keen Derrick joining him in the front compartment of a much-used old desert truck, both men were driven away with the bearded Bedouin's who had accompanied Akmer to Karl's hotel room, to arrive jerkily, with grinding gears and rasping brakes at Al Ghazzawi's camp, where the little round man sat as before on his pile of cushions. He arose and embraced Karl and Derrick, then sent for his daughter, Leda, to come over to the men's side of the tent.

She entered from behind the cloth curtain, wearing flimsy midnight blue veils and a silk light blue robe. Her long tawny hair was loosely tied back with ribbon, whilst shorter strands escaped, framing her narrow face. She looked majestic and beautiful, and a little bit like her brother, Akmer.

Karl could see the likeness now.

She immediately walked across to Derrick and embraced him.

"Ah, my boyfriend has returned!" There was a twinkle in her eye. It was her turn to make Derrick look embarrassed, but she said it with good humour, and he realised she was not only joking, but playfully getting her own back!

"Leda will introduce you to the women of my camp, Karl, and I hope they will not be too hard on you!" Al Ghazzawi chuckled gleefully at his daughter's intervention.

"It was I who asked for the transformation!" Karl grinned at Leda, and cheerfully indicated the cloth curtain behind which he knew the women of the camp were waiting for him.

"Lead me on Leda!" He ordered, and the young maid dimpled, her exotic antimony outlined eyes sparkled at him, reflecting her pleasure.

# ABU DHABI. CUNNING MOVES

As Al Ghazzawi had surmised about his son, Asad had indeed compiled a list of contacts, who he was even now phoning on his pure golden mobile which lay beside his antique gold phone, whose bottom rested solidly on a gilt-inlaid ebony occasional table. Asad's room was full of delicate gold antiques and stunning pictures of framed art which he'd amassed secretly and privately via unorthodox means. The antiquities he had arranged around his room were prohibited goods; they arrived under shady deals, and had certainly bypassed the sharp eyes of customs officials!

He had lists for gun-runners, slave traders, shady oil dealers, crooked antique dealers, dishonest archaeological dealers – and a list of sex traffickers. He was calling these on the latter sheet now.

"Greetings, Saki. I bring you good news! I have three females you might be interested in!"

He phoned several men who expressed a wish to see 'the females'. Then he sat back to have his meal, dreaming of making a deal soon – one in England with Paul Wright, and one here.

Then he noticed he'd missed someone out whose name was on his list...

"Ramuth Soukis? I don't recall him? Must be a new dealer! Can't think why I've not heard of him before! His is a Bedu name! I think I'll include him at my private gathering, to crow over what I have to show the others...his achievements in the underworld are impeccable, and he appears to have the perfect crooked contacts! Yes, he'll be contacted!"

# LONDON. POLICE VISIT

"That's it! It's three o'clock, and I've just called Fran, but am getting only voice mail. Something has happened to her! We must go to the police, Nigel. I can't wait another moment!"

Nigel was worried as well. "Right, luv, I'll get the car out again!"

They drove to the nearest station, which was just a couple of blocks away, two anxious people,

puzzled and concerned for Fran.

The stern-looking Operative behind the enquiry desk, heard the worry in their voices and paid them the attention he felt they deserved.

"Missing, you say? I'll make a note of it and give you a crime number. Have you a recent picture of your daughter?"

Mandy rummaged in her handbag. "It's here, somewhere! I must have a clear-out! Oh yes, here it is." As she pulled the picture from her bag it was unexpectedly snatched from her hand.

"Here, give my photo back!"

The man she addressed was perhaps near retirement age. He had a shock of white hair, and wore a dark-coloured suit with a dashing striped tie. The man smiled politely at her: "I'm sorry to alarm you, but did I hear you say your daughter was missing, Mrs..?"

"Mrs Tompkins, yes, she is! Since last night. She was supposed to be coming round today, but she didn't and –"

"Can I borrow this photograph?" The man in the suit studied Fran's photo. He seemed to be taking this very seriously. Mandy glanced at her husband, who shrugged.

"I suppose so... Who are you?"

"I'm DCI John Denby. Look, come up to the office with me. I need to check the police computer.

Tell me your story on the way!"

There were two chairs in John's office, tucked away in an untidy corner, and he bade Mandy and Nigel to sit in them until he came back.

Mandy looked about her in awe. "I didn't think we'd get this far! I've never been in a police station before!"

"I have!"

She looked at her husband in surprise. "When was that? You've never told me! What ever did you do wrong?"

Nigel's foot scuffed the lino floor. He coloured slightly. "Nothing too bad! It was a long time ago, dear – before we even met!"

"Why, Nigel, I didn't realise you were such a hoodlum in your hey-day!" Mandy gently chided him, grinning at his discomfort.

John, meanwhile, was checking with his supervising Operative. "They are the only people, so far, who've come in about a missing daughter!" He waved the snapshot of Fran in front of his superior's dead-pan face. "I'm sure she's the other girl! Sure of it!"

"Hold your horses, John! What other girl?"

"The one I told you about earlier – the kidnapping job."

"Oh, that one. Have you checked the most recently missing on the database?"

"I just have. There's no one on it that looks like her, and she lives in London, where the other girl was taken."

"Leave this with me, John. I'll check with the Met –"

"It's on our patch, Sir!"

"I know, but just in case, let's make it hush hush for the time being! Are the girls parents still here?"

"Sitting in my office."

"Tell them we'll do what we can, but no reporters. I don't want this blowing up in our face when we know bugger all yet. Got it?"

"I suppose so."

"I'm not sure you do, John."

"Yeah, okay. I get it. I've got to twiddle my bloody thumbs whilst you go through the diplomatic channels." John sighed heavily, heartily wishing for less red tape so he could thoroughly investigate this incident. He had a gut feeling it would be worth his time and patience! It was his last year before retirement and a case like this would boost his moral and earn him an immortal place in police history! He could picture the newspaper tabloids with his grinning picture splashed over the front page showering him with success he'd always hoped to achieve in his dogged, hard-working job!

# ABU DHABI. BACK TO THE DESERT

If he thought he'd relished the hospitality of Farid Al Ghazzawi's tent on the men's side, then Karl had to admit that the women's quarters were even more enjoyable and luxurious, even though they all lived out on the sand!

Only the married women served him, first by giving him a simple meal of bread baked in the hot sand, more rice dates, followed by yoghurt and foamy milk straight from the camel. The milk tasted warm and sweet, yet was refreshing.

After the meal, he lay on colourful cushions and rich, thick hand-embroidered carpets, made by these desert women, and allowed the married ladies to sponge him down in warm scented rosewater, joining in their hilarity, and unashamedly grinning at their rich, saucy remarks over his exposed, half-nude body. They did not realise he understood some of their language! They carefully massaged his muscular chest and arms in a perfumed oil that smelt of Myrrh and Tuberose, still giggling away amongst themselves, while Al Ghazzawi's daring daughter, (and some other young maidens), surveyed these exhilarating proceedings through a gap in the tent walls of the woman's quarters, hiding their own admiring smiles!

Their further administrations afterwards were rough, awkward and time-consuming, but he bore it all with good humour, knowing the end would justify the means. When he was done, they left him in peace.

The scintillating scent and oils had made him drowsy, so he managed a catnap again, awakening to full alert within fifteen minutes or so. He felt better for this frivolous attention; he was alive and ready for whatever the remaining evening should bring.

It brought an anticipated phone call. "Would Mister so-so like to attend –?" It was a little distorted, the signal weak, but he knew who it had come from, and why. Casually, he accepted the invite, pleased part of his plan had worked, and snapped his mobile off. Then he thanked all the women around him for their ablutions. For all he knew this could be his last night on Earth, but he had enjoyed most of the preparation he'd undergone. Although, what had been done to him felt strange. He was prepared now, his plan clear in his mind, and had no regrets; he had made peace with his God long ago when it came to dangerous liaisons, as he'd told Dickie.

A while later he walked along the sand dunes with the seductive Leda, leaving ex-squadron leader and work-mentor Dickie, to enjoy Al Ghazzawi's Bedouin hospitality. The tribal leader immediately clapped for some desert wine for his exalted guest, and instructed a thick shawl to be given to Dickie to wear over his navy cardigan. "We must look after our victorious saviours!" He spoke with respect, when Derrick thanked him. "But I will not have wine until later, not 'till we come back!"

The sweet drink offered to Dickie tasted like a kind of syrupy sherry. It was heart-warming and delicious. He sipped his rich alcoholic solution slowly. He realised he was also enjoying this talkative Bedouin's amazing company and hospitality. He asked Al Ghazzawi innocently: "What happens now, my friend?"

"Alas, I will leave you, shortly. We're making ready for our ghazwas, after which. all will be revealed to you! I can say no more. Karl wishes it so."

"I have been his mentor for several years. I know him well. He's off on some 'action plan' of his, isn't he?"

Al Ghazzawi shot Derrick a shrewd look, and nodded slightly, weighing up certain possibilities, wondering if he should tell more tit-bits of information to this retired, solid-looking Englishman, who had so bravely helped win the war for his country.

Derrick sensed he was getting close to cracking Karl's

secret plan. He could be very persuasive when he wanted to be, and said subtly. "Confidentially of course, you wouldn't be the first man to talk about what Karl is attempting to do, and I ask this as a...friend?"

Al Ghazzawi guffawed at his attempt, and winked heavily...

As they walked slowly through the camp, Leda said airily: "Your friend, the airman, I sense he is a good person."

"Yeah, he's one of the best. I've worked with him on the force. He's wise, helpful and loyal! We've been friends ever since we've known each other!"

"What did you do when you knew Mr Derrick?"

"I was in the RAF for a spell, as a mechanic – hence meeting Dickie. Then I joined the police... pretty much what I'm doing now, protecting people and rescuing them from the bad guys."

"You make it sound so easy. Yet it can't be all plain sailing? Isn't that how you say it?"

Karl smiled, "Sure, I sail with the wind!" he joked, as Leda laughed lightly at his weak pun. He added, seriously: "No, you're right, it isn't. It's rough, tough, and dangerous. Take tonight, I wonder if you know what your father and I are up too later this evening?"

A playful note entered Leda's voice: "You're certainly not attending a party together, dressed so dangerously! Nor are any of our men! It's intriguing!" But she considered her thoughts before she said. "We women are not told much; but the men are busy tonight. Some have been cleaning their rifles, whilst others have gone away on mysterious errands. I think our men are making ready for a ghazwas?"

"Maybe, or maybe something else. How do I look?"

She grinned at his majestic stance admiringly. "Very striking! Very different!"

He flashed her a grin from white, perfect teeth. She noticed a line of scar-tissue by his mouth, and couldn't resist tracing the line of the scar with her finger. "A dagger, Mr Karl?"

"A knife...I live on the edge! It was made by an assassin in Cairo whom I had to fight!"

"I like men who 'live on the edge'! Did you killed the assassin, or did he get away?"

"Yeah, I had to – it was him or me! You really are a true Bedouin woman! Your people breathe fire and spirit, and you love stories about adventure, don't you?"

"Of course! I have adventurous blood! As a tom-boy of this tribe, I was always getting into scrapes in the desert! My father sent my brothers to help me fight my battles with the scorpions and snakes! And I was always playing tricks on my people through non-poisonous insects!"

"I cannot see you as a tom-boy, somehow...!"

"Oh, believe me – I was a little monster!"

"...I see you as a lovely woman."

Leda dimpled, her hazel eyes seemed to melt. "Thank you. I am so used to my people calling me the 'devil child' when I was younger, it makes a change to receive a compliment!"

Karl smiled. "It makes me feel good to give one! It seems we have both had some 'adventures'!"

"Tonight is an adventure for my father, is it not?"

"Yes."

"Take care of him. His family and his people love him very much."

"He will take care of himself, don't worry, little sister."

"So, I'm a little sister, am I? I'm not so little that I cannot ask you to kiss me!"

Karl stopped walking and stared at her in surprise. She was irresistible! To kiss her now went against all his principles; he had firmly told Tanja he didn't want to be tied, but this Bedouin woman's warm and bright company dimmed his wary emotions. She dimpled at him almost coyly.

They had moved further from the eyes of the camp by now, but even so, he spoke carefully: "I wouldn't want you to get into trouble with the authorities. Isn't it a forbidden law to kiss in public? We are not even married!"

"Yes – true! But we are alone, there is only the desert to watch over us. I challenge you to kiss me!  I think you would like to!"

So he kissed her – properly. When he released her, she said, in a relaxed, casual way: "Now you will have to marry me!"

He rolled his eyes, thinking she was teasing him. "Do you always do this to stranger's in your camp? Is that traditional? I wouldn't mind marrying you, actually!"

"Are you teasing me now? Our laws are so finicky where love and marriage is concerned!"

Karl nodded. "I know that.  But this place is really something! I could live the life you lead!"

She smirked, her eyes lively: "With me, Englishman? Is that a proposal?"

"It's kind of like one." He hesitated, the words came out before he could stop them. He felt a heel after what he'd said to Tanja, but this woman was so alluring! "Perhaps, after tonight, I may see you again?"

"I would like that. Come back safely." She stepped away and surveyed him, seriously this time. In the end, she said: "You look very different. But I would be proud to call you a boyfriend!"

She was forthright.  It seemed they had come to an understanding.  Karl went to put his arm around her shoulders, but she shrugged him off with a warning finger; they were almost back at camp and must not be seen loitering in the sands together!  He complied, not wanting to cause her any trouble.

As they continued walking, she asked: "Have you a girlfriend at the moment?"

Again, he thought of Tanja and Kimmi, wondering what was happening to them. "Not exactly, no.  There were people from my past. What about you? Any men friends?"

She laughed at his question. "Plenty of admirers! I may search for someone special one day!

But you intrigue me... Tell me more about your adventures!"

"Later on, we're back now and it will soon be time for me to go! It's getting dark!"

# LONDON. WARNED OFF!

John Denby was at home when his phone rang. He took the call in his study. It was his superior Operative.

"Hi, John."

"Hi, sir. What can I do for you?"

"Just thought you'd want to know... I've had an interesting call."

"Oh?"

"Yes. Not from the Met, but from the Criminal Intelligence Unit Special Ops!

"CIUSO?"

"Yeah. The buggers have warned us off your kidnap case!"

"Are you sure? I mean – why the hell Special Ops? What's going on?"

"Zilch! Nothing, as far as we're concerned. We're out of it! Sorry, John, I know you liked this one, but the other blighter's have got it first!"

"You mean, we can't do a thing?"

"We're not allowed to tread on the Big Boy's toes – their express orders. Just letting you know! Sorry, John. See you Monday."

John blew his cheeks out. Bloody hell! He was all set to handle this case! He sighed heavily, life just wasn't fair!

His phone rang again. "Hallo?"

"John? Hi, it's Ben Elliston. Any news on the kidnap drama? Are you going to take it on?"

"I can't. We've been warned off taking it by the Criminal Intelligence Unit Special Ops, would you believe!"

"The CIUSO? Can they do this? Swear you to secrecy – that sort of thing?"

"'Fraid so! They're the hotshots! My hands are tied. Sorry, Ben."

"As MP I had high hopes you'd be able to help Paul Wright in my constituency, but I was wrong. Oh well, thanks for trying. Can you tell me who is stopping you?"

"My superior! He's had direct orders from higher up the chain, at CIUSO!"

"So you can't intervene?"

"No! Much as I'd like too!"

"A shame!" There followed a deep sigh from the other end. "I can't pull any strings here, then? I don't like this, the CIUSO involved! As you say, they're the tops! Against my better judgement, we'll have to leave it!"

"Yeah, Ben, thanks for telling me about it! I'll keep the incident in mind, just in case anything changes."

"Thanks. You're not a bad cop, John! You would have got things moving for Paul – poor, worried blighter!"

# ABU DHABI. MOVEMENT

"I don't believe this, you say we have to change back into our old clothes now? Whatever for?"

Both girls were astonished at Emir's sudden order.

"Do this!" Leigh continued, her hands on her hips in a pouting stance. "Do that! I'm sick of it!"

Emir produced his gun and waved it at her.

Fran spoke warningly: "Leigh!"

"He won't shoot me! I'm too valuable!"

Emir said: "I may not shoot you, but I can certainly stop your dinner from coming. It is ready."

"I don't want it!" Leigh was near to tears again.

Fran crossed over and grabbed her friend's hand. She squeezed it. "I know how you feel, but we must eat, to keep our strength up!"

Leigh collapsed against her, all in. "Oh, all right! But why the clothes change – I didn't even bother to hang mine up!"

Emir said: "'Why' is not relevant. My master has his reasons."

"And where's my mother gone? Why haven't you left her here with us?"

Emir murmured: "All will be revealed. Now, change quickly, and Ameen will bring your food."

When he'd left, Leigh groaned: "I don't think I can eat any more rich Arab stuff! I want a

MacDonald's! Bet they've got one out here! Your looking worried, Fran. Why?"

"Just wondering what Boulos is up to!"

Leigh caught her friend's pensive mood. "It's something bad, I'll bet!"

As both girls changed back into their party frocks,

Leigh complained: "Mine stinks of stale perfume and spilt drink! Ugh! I hate wearing clothes that are dirty, it makes me feel unclean and horrible!"

"We've no choice." Fran soothed her automatically, recognising her friend's building hysteria.

Leigh must not crack up now. Fran, herself, was having trouble worrying what the future held for her!

Ameen entered their room, bearing a tray of appetising finger dishes. Despite their fears, the girls ate their meal quickly and quietly, as though it was their last one. To their surprise Ameen had brought them each a large glass of red wine.

"That's odd!" Leigh exclaimed, but drank hers anyway. Fran left her glass untouched. She sipped at the water Ameen had also provided them with.

"Don't you like red?" Leigh asked Fran.

"Er, no."

"Can I have yours?"

"I left mine in case it was spiked."

Leigh looked thunderstruck. "Oh bloody hell – I didn't think!"

"It's okay. I don't think they'd try to dope us again. Keep calm, Leigh."

"I'm going to puke!"

"No you're not! Just take deep breaths."

Ameen entered to take their dishes away. Leigh purposefully strode up to him.

"What did you put in my drink, you git!"

Fran tried to hold her friend's arm. Ameen raised his gun, looking surprised at Leigh's fury.

"Sit down! Sit! Sit!"

"How dare you poison me! You're all against us, you dark, dirty sods! You should all be shot, not me!" Leigh's mounting hysteria had escaped.

Ameen raised his hand and struck her across the face before Fran could do anything.

"Oh, oh, aagh!" Leigh screamed, her hand instinctively moving to her features. When she took it away there appeared a livid red mark on her white cheek.

Fran rushed to her side. She said quickly, to Ameen. "You didn't have to do that! I'll look after her! Can't you see she's distraught! Give us space for a minute!"

Ameen shook his head. "We go, now – now! My master has ordered that it be so!"

"Blow your master!" Even Fran was angry at this point.

"What's going on?"Asked a female voice, and Fran spun towards the door to see Serena being ushered into the room by Emir, who was carrying his gun as usual.

Serena looked pale, but calm. She had changed into a revealing, all-in-one black cat-suit and silver high heels.

Ameen blustered, eyeing Serena with hard, dark eyes: "Your daughter is behaving badly!"

"I'm not surprised!" Serena was unruffled. "It isn't every day us girls get kidnapped!"

She bought some degree of levity to the tense situation. Fran noticed Leigh was calming down, her hand still drawn to her cheek. Leigh said tremblingly: "No ones ever hit me before!"

Fran's kind heart went out to her. She hugged her friend whilst Serena kept a watchful distance, keeping any natural, maternal emotions for Leigh under wraps. Fran angrily shook her rueful head over the woman's laid-back attitude towards her only daughter, wishing Serena would show some motherly concern for the shocked girl.

Emir waved his gun at them again. "We go, now! Our master is waiting!"

In trepidation, Serena and the two girls filed out, reluctant to leave their snow-white bedroom. It had become their bolt-hole, their little haven of uneasy safety....

# ABU DHABI. A MYSTERY GUEST

It was now about eight thirty in the evening in UAE Standard Time. Asad's lounge was brightly lit and the large, luxurious blinds were tightly closed, hiding the city view from the penthouse's wide, scenic windows. There were four other men in the room as well as Asad Boulos, and they were all awaiting the women's entrance with keen interest...

One man, with dark hair and lean beard looked of European descent, and he wore a light blue summer suit with a white, open-necked shirt. His thin fingers were covered in gold rings of elegant design, and he looked as if he had just come from a business meeting, for he carried a bulging brown briefcase beside him. Of all the men he looked the most decent.

Two other men, both wealthy Arabs, wore the usual white thobe and headdress. One was fat with hairy arms whilst the other was fairly thin. He wore dark, orb-like glasses.

The fourth man was lounging casually on one of the plush white armchairs. Asad had introduced him to the other men, saying: "Gentlemen, this is Ramuth Soukis, a Bedu by birth. He is new to our market. I brought him in because he has such excellent credentials, and I hope he will spend all his money on us!"

There was a general laugh amongst the men, and Soukis speared them all with a quick, careful smirk, as if he was afraid to smile openly.

He was wearing dark and dusty attire which consisted of open-toed old leather sandals, a black thobe, and a wide, floppy hood that covered most of his face. He also wore an eye-patch which made him look like a devious and dangerous savage. He had an off-hand, haughty demeanour.

Out of curiosity Asad spoke civilly to Soukis, in Arabic, probably thinking the other man might speak back to him in Modern Hebrew, or Amharic, as Bedouin's were known to speak in several dialects: "As a Bedouin, how have you managed to prosper so well? This is our Inner Circle; we keep each other's secrets safe. What you say here will go no further than this room! You haven't told me yet, what is your line of business, may I ask?"

Soukis replied shortly, in throaty Arabic. "Camel racing!" His good eye noticed the twitchy mouths and snooty raised eyebrows of the other men. Ignoring their undisguised distaste, he added: "Much money can be found in it – especially if you can smuggle illegal goods in, between the lines!"

"Ah! A man after my own heart! You smuggle, huh? And now you have turned to something a little different, a little more...exotic, shall we say? But women are pricey, my friend! Can you afford what I offer here, this evening?"

Soukis's voice roughened, as if he was insulted by Asad's silky tone. "Do you think me a fool to arrive empty-handed? I have all the money in the world!"

"Not at all!" Asad spread out his chubby, well-polished fingers at Soukis. "I merely ask this because you are new here! These men whom I know, naturally, want to hear more about you, or they may become suspicious of your intentions!"

Soukis expanded his chest, and thundered: "My intentions are honourable! I may not be so well-dressed as you are, but my status is not so downtrodden as you all think! I am no humble-class Bedu! I am insulted! I shall leave, and take my money elsewhere!"

"Wait, Ramuth! Let me rephrase my words! You cannot leave my hospitality on such a sour note!"

"Then I may reconsider... If you give me an apology!"

Asad hesitated, not wanting to demean himself to this haughty man in front of his guests. He was beginning to wish he hadn't invited him! But the idea of making more money and striking rich deals was too inviting to ignore! He knew he would be lucky tonight! Plus, soon, he would have Paul Wright's ransom money to contend with. He could afford to be magnanimous to this dour, offensive Bedouin!

The fat Arab, who had been standing near to Soukis, growled impatiently in Arabic: "You waste time, Asad! I cannot stay long! I go to another meeting in half-an-hour!"

The thin Arab, who had arrived with the fat one cried out fiercely, in his tongue: "No! Asad is right to ask Ramuth Soukis these questions! I do not trust newcomers who may not rise to our standards, we are paying BIG money here! I warn you – I will easily outbid this man, and he will be ashamed that he came!"

Asad glanced a little uneasily at Soukis; how would this untidy, cloak-swirling Bedouin take the thin man's rude report? The group he'd invited tonight were usually more relaxed, polite and charming than this! Had he made a vital mistake including this dour Arab into his exclusive circle of contacts?

Ramuth Soukis looked down his nose at the thin Arab. "You rich millionaires, sporting fast, status-symbol cars, you all live so softly! I bargain hard! It is you who will be ashamed when you come away empty-handed!" He glared at Asad Boulos. "I want my apology, or I go!"

"Gentlemen, let us not get heated! I had to sound you out, Ramuth, don't be hasty! I urge you to stay. Sorry if I offended you!"

Soukis inclined his head, accepting the apology with a swirling wave from beneath his cloak.

The fat Arab scowled. "Can we get on with it now? I'm sorry to insist so forcefully, Asad, but I really have to leave soon!"

The European man in the smart city suit had not said anything during this interchange, now he glanced pointedly at his gold wristwatch and gave a quiet sigh.

Asad noticed. "I will send for the ladies, be patient,

gentlemen! In the meantime, let us have some champaign!" He opened an expensive embossed bottle with a practised flourish, and began to pour, waiting on his guests himself.

Ramuth Soukis said proudly: "I will not sup with you! This is women's drink! It is against my religion!"

Asad wanted to scream at the man; he was getting everyone's back up! Politely, and carefully he asked: "Would you accept a different form of alcohol, or even a coke, Ramuth?"

"Just desalinated water!" Replied the stone-faced camel racer abruptly, seemingly unaware he'd raised any tension in the room.

Asad stopped serving the drinks and clapped his hands. Emir and Ameen entered the lounge with a curious Serena and the scared, unwilling girls in tow.

All the men were watching the girls in a way that made Leigh and Fran shiver with apprehension.

Soukis squinted at them carefully. The girls tried to give him a wide berth; they didn't like the look of him on sight. Even the wary Serena stepped cautiously away from him!

Soukis's good eye darted meaningfully towards the expectant Asad. He ordered: "My eyes are not so good; tell them to come here, to me!"

"But, of course – whatever you wish!" Asad almost rubbed his hands in pleasure at seeing the girls again. "Go stand by Ramuth!" He ordered them.

Reluctantly, all three women moved to where he indicated.

Leigh opened her mouth to say something, but her mother unkindly nudged her shoulder and the bemused girl had no choice but to remain silent.

"This is good!" Asad beamed at the men, still speaking in Arabic. "What do you think of the girls, eh?"

The fat man, and the thin one spoke at once, excitedly asking something in the Arab tongue, eyeing the girls greedily as if they were buried treasure. Asad answered them rapidly, seeming to tick off certain points on his fingers, gesticulating confidently at the girls in an airy, self-assured manner, for the two Arab men had started to talk of costs. The girls didn't have a clue what was going on, but Serena, who understood some basic words, showed a stony face. Leigh copied her mother's expression, and Fran looked scared.

Soukis had been listening, intently studying the girls, coiled like a silent snake in his armchair. He suddenly stood up and strode to where Fran was standing. She shrunk back from him, but he caught a lock of her hair, and wonderingly trickled his fingers through her tumbled curls. Fran shuddered at his touch, feeling his grimy fingers catching in her uncombed locks, and hoping this wouldn't happen again! What was it about her dishevelled hair that attracted these Arab men to do this to her? Soukis said something to Asad in Arabic, which made Asad's eyes light up, just as the man in the suit also spoke out: "I am interested in all of them, Asad!"

"That is good news for me, Peta!" Asad's bright eyes swerved from Soukis to the suited Peta in keen anticipation.

"I am interested too," Soukis said simply. His one, good eye locked with those of the suited man and held his gaze in a daring way. "I warn you! Do not underestimate me!" He spoke deliberately to Peta. "I spend with hard cash!"

Peta glared back at the uncouth Soukis. "So do I!" He patted his bulging briefcase. Straight away, he named a price outright.

To the astonished girls eyes, who were unaware of the language being spoken, there seemed to be a battle going on between the two men; they both became verbally excited, pointing at the girls as if some duel was taking place in the elegant white and gold sitting room.

The other two Arabs had stopped their banter in wary disbelief; the price was sky-rocketing out of control! They both knew when to admit defeat, and were ungraciously preparing to leave.

The girls were mystified, but Serena's expression grew stonier and stonier. At one point, she frowned hard, and tried to speak. "Asad, you can't do this to m —" She pleaded.

"Quiet, madam," he said, warningly. "We are in the middle of a decent discussion – pray, carry on gentlemen!"

"You bastard!" Serena spoke quickly, before Emir's gun came into play and he covered her with it.

"What is happening, mother?"

Serena eyed the gun with burning eyes. "Nothing!" She muttered, mutinously.

It was Fran's turn to look equally upset. "I think the swine is selling us to the highest bidder!"

Leigh's mouth dropped open in shock. "Their bidding for us? Boulos can't do this – my father –!"

"Listen daughter, Asad will take the ransom money and everything else off our backs – I've been stupidly taken in as much as you two by him, the greedy sod!" Her mother spat out, glaring at the duplicitous Arab.

Asad shot her a caressingly familiar yet disarming grin. "You can't win them all, my dear Serena! Life has to move on!"

"Mother! What do you mean? Do you know this man?"

But Serena clamped her lips together, suddenly realising she'd said too much. Her eyes glittered with angry tears.

Leigh was glaring at her mother, her senses sharpened to an acute point. She said, furiously: "You always have to have a man around, don't you! Don't tell me you've taken up with that thug! That Boulos thing! He's dropped you, hasn't he? Hasn't he?"

Serena took a deep breath, turning away from her daughters smug, challenging stare. She took up an unconcerned stance and shrugged, saying lightly: "Why should you care? Are you jealous because you're a daddy's girl and you haven't got a man?"

"Ahhh – you bitch-of-a-mother!" Leigh howled. She had forgotten the gun; her hand lashed out and her fingernails raked the side of Serena's face.

The men had stopped their talk and were glancing uneasily at the enraged Leigh. Fran took time to notice that

Asad Boulos was looking pleased with himself.

"The bugger's sold us!" She thought to herself, and a little spurt of anger began to grow inside her.

"The devious sod!"

She then noticed more clearly that the fat man and thin man had left the apartment, sweeping out with bowed shoulders, yet with their heads held high in disgust. Which left Soukis in devilish garbs, and Peta remaining in the elegant lounge.

Asad was giving his orders to Emir: "Take the girls back to their room and lock them in. I don't want them escaping now, when I'm so close to victory!"

He actually rubbed his hands and said lightly, to the face-scarred Serena in the girls hearing, having seen the altercation of emotion that had taken place between herself and her daughter: "Never mind, Serena. I couldn't have kept up the pretence any longer! You were two old for me!"

To which Serena raised two fingers in the air in an unladylike gesture, but her tight, slightly-lined wan face showed her distress only too clearly. Deep down, she was scarred by his betrayal.

Fran actually found herself feeling sorry for the woman who was trying, gamely, to hold herself together. She was one tough bird, thought the girl, a certain admiration for Serena was creeping in...

All Emir's and Ameen's attention were on herding the helpless, distraught Serena and the girls back to their room, in an awed, this-can't-be-happening, despairing way. Asad, grinning fiendishly, had helped himself to more champaign.

Suddenly, the apartment's double, red-coated entry door was urgently blasted wide open, as if a magic spring had been sprung, and men quickly poured into Asad's lounge carrying loaded rifles. The sudden change was momentous. Asad dropped his decorated champaign glass in shock, whilst Emir and Ameen didn't even have time to use their weapons, but froze on the spot, surrounded by dark-robed Bedouin's. The small puff of smoke made by the unhinged front doors had the girls screaming at the black hooded figures, and even Serena looked terrified at all the men with their rifles scurrying with purpose into the room. The whole, unexpected tableau seemed menacing to them! From above the unhinged door an alarm bell was ringing, protecting Asad's treasures against theft, but it was turned off, mysteriously, by an unknown hand, as suddenly as it had started, and no hotel staff, security men, or police came running to see what was amiss, for the penthouse was situated adjacent and higher up to the actual hotel, and was virtually separate from it.

The intruders immediately forced Emir and Ameen to surrender their guns. Reluctantly, they had to lay their hand-guns down at an order shouted to them in their own language. They held their hands upon their heads in astonished surrender and were frisked quickly, before being sullenly led out of the lounge at gunpoint, without a word being said by either of them.

Whilst this was going on, unknowingly, Asad had drawn a small pistol from his robes...

But Peta, hot from negotiating for the three women, noticed. He suddenly dived at Asad without reason, raising his arm to strike at the duplicitous Arab. Asad Boulos fired at him quickly in defence. The girls screamed again as the suited man staggered backwards, hugging a shattered shoulder where the blood blossomed instantly, seeping through his fingers and down the arm of his light blue suit.

Some of the wild-looking Bedouin's with their rifles held casually, gathered around the shot man and helped support him to lie on some cushions from the sofa, which they laid on the flanked, shiny, cool wooden floor. At the same time, Soukis, of the dark greasy clothes and eye-piece had edged closer to Asad, and he jumped him, grabbing the Arab's gun arm. To the girls horror, both men tried to gain supremacy of the weapon, whilst the remaining men with rifles, unperturbed, watched the fight!

As the frightened girls gasped, cowed by the violence, Soukis punched Asad Boulos square on the nose. Asad grunted and dropped the pistol. He returned the assault with a right-handed blow, but his assailant moved quickly aside for one in heavy garbs, and Asad's raging fist swiped through empty space. As Asad managed to steady himself, his hand came out and somehow, clutched hold of the other man's robe. Boulos pulled, hard, and the two men crashed together, and he's grasping hands found the other man's neck, and he began to squeeze in earnest determination...

His slim, silver pistol had slithered across the floor on the polished wood. It was now or never. Fran bent down and swooped up the weapon. Calmly and expertly, she checked the release catch and aimed it at Asad in a two-handed stance, ready to fire.

Leigh and Serena gaped at her in utter amazement as she cried: "STOP! I have a gun on you! In the name of Criminal Intelligence Unit Special Ops, resist me, and I will have the greatest pleasure in shooting you, Asad Boulos!"

# ABU DHABI. HOME-TRUTHS

Everyone gaped at the girl in the crumpled black dress and untidy blond hair as she held the pistol steadily in her hands, her demeanour calm, but cold. Even the men with the rifles were taken by surprise, and had their weapons only half raised, too staggered by the turn of events to react as quickly as they should.

Asad didn't pause, but acted quickly; he pulled Soukis in front of him, like a shield, and wrenched the man's shoulder up behind his back.

"Go ahead you two-faced bitch – whoever you are – Soukis is my passport out of here!" He began to edge away, with his assailant awkwardly shuffling with him.

Fran didn't waste a second; she sighted, and fired. Asad was mostly hidden behind Soukis, but a leg was in view and Fran's bullet hit his leg. Asad screamed, his limb buckling under him, and as he went down, he let go of Soukis, who moved away quickly from danger. Soukis spoke to Fran encouragingly across the crowded room – but not in Arabic as she had expected.

Soukis said to her in normal English: "Well done, Fran! You've saved us all!"

Fran started from her poised stance and stared hard, with narrowed, gimlet eyes at the grimy, robe-strewn stranger with the evil-looking eye-patch. Then she smiled. "I might have known you'd be in disguise! I certainly didn't recognise you! You look fatter!"

"Under all these drapes I'm wearing a bullet-proof vest!"

Having said this, and surprised everyone but Fran, to Leigh and Serena's frightened amazement, the man with the eye-patch took off his headdress and eye-mask with a flourish, and revealed himself.

Leigh stared at him, unable to believe her eyes. "You!" She breathed, thoroughly startled.

"Yes, me! Your dance companion of last night – Karl Silverman!"

Asad Boulos cranked his chin up sharply on hearing Karl's name stated. He stared in total disbelief from his pained position on the floor, glaring hard at the English speaking Operative, so striking and evil-looking in his dark, swirly Arabian shirt and cloak. Asad found his voice and spoke in English. "YOU! Karl Silverman! The man I was warned about? How did you manage this masquerade? I would never have guessed you were an Englishman! How did such false papers naming you as Ramouth Soukis get into my Penthouse? I was totally taken in by you!"

"They were planted – by Peta's people, working undercover with us! Your alarm system is not so good as you thought it was!"

Asad shuffled his good foot on the floor in temper. "Peta has been coming to my secret meetings for some time – I trusted him as a confidential ally! But his papers must have been forged, by you I suppose! I was a vain fool – I should have had you shot when you got here!"

Then, he remembered something; a cunning grin replaced the pain on his face. "Ah! But I hold the wildcard! By a certain friend's orders, your people were taken somewhere in England! I know where your girlfriend and her daughter are held!"

"I have no doubt you do – you felon!" In his rough clothes, Karl bent down to Asad's crafty face.

"It would give me the greatest pleasure to crush you, you insolent dog! Where are they?"

"Ah! Have I drawn blood?" Asad sneered at Karl's taut expression. "I have you over a barrel, Englishman! But you must grant me a handsome favour in return!" He waved at the Bedouin's surrounding him with their weapons. "Call these nomad's off, bind my bloody leg, and allow me to escape! I will tell you where your people are!"

"No deal!"

"If your people are so precious to you, I think you'll do as I ask, or they will be killed by my men, and you'll have their death's on your conscience for evermore! Do you really want that?"

"What I want," Karl grated, "is to have you under lock and key, charged heavily with your dirty crimes, you insidious bastard, where you can do no more harm to innocent people!"

"But look what harm you can do to your people!" Boulos cunningly pointed out. "When the men in England realise something has happened to me, they will act according to my instructions! Understand this: never again will your friends see the sun, nor the moon by night! You have been warned, Englishman! The path of the wind waits for no one. What will it be service man, your woman and child alive, or their death's at my orders? The choice is yours."

"Save your bluster. I don't tolerate your proposal!"

"Is that a 'no'?"

"It is."

"Then you will never see your loved ones again!" Asad warned darkly.

Karl knew he was right, but he would not be goaded by this man's threats, worried as he was about Tanja and Kimmi.

"You forget; we are fours hours ahead of British Time, it should be enough to sort you and your cronies out. I'm going to take that risk!"

"If I should be charged, there are those in England who know what to do!" Asad insisted, realising he was losing this argument.

"We know about those in England! You can't escape our net as easily as you think; I have a surprise for you outside! Some people you've evaded for a long, long time!"

"What surprise?"

"The Abu Dhabi police are waiting to take you away... Which reminds me, I must see to Peta!"

Asad's entreating face changed, his soft lips bared to a snarl and he spat on the floor, his thin veneer of assumed respectability had worn thin, showing him up for all to see as the callous thug he really was. He vented his raw feelings in a tirade of Arabic abuse at Karl's stubborn pig-headedness. He was no longer the rich, upright, gambling and chancing gentleman the world knew him as. Even if the British Operative arrested him now, he realised too late, that by Arab law he would be dealt with severely, probably even before he got to Britain. It hit home, and he became silent, and bowed his wavy head...

Karl headed over to the wounded man lying on the floor. He spoke in Arabic. "Can you hold up, Peta? I believe someone has sent for an ambulance!"

"I'm not hurt too badly, Karl!" Peta grunted, holding his bloody shoulder with his good arm. "The Bedu's are looking after me! You've helped the Abu Dhabi police no end, they'll probably recommend you to one of our higher governors! I'll speak well for you!"

"Thanks!"

Karl turned to one of the girls. "I'm sorry you had to go through all this." He spoke to Leigh, who was staring at him, dry-mouthed, wondering why Karl was talking to a would-be slave trader so personally! Hadn't the shot man on the floor wanted to buy them? She couldn't take it in!

"It's been too much!" Mumbled a weary Leigh. "What on earth are you doing here, and how...?"

She spun around to Fran. "Fran, I never guessed. You – your from Special Ops you say? Who the hell are they? How come?"

"We're an elite police group. It was a set-up," Fran explained, "to catch Asad Boulos in the act. Me and Karl worked separately on Boulos's criminal profile. He is wanted by both the Abu Dhabi police and our British CIUSO department."

"Other explanations will have to wait!" Karl looked down at the groaning Asad. He'd caught sight of someone else entering the room, and now he said to Asad Boulos:

"You'll have to moan in pain a bit longer – you have an important visitor who is eager to see you!"

Asad raised his pained face to find a man staring fixedly at him, with his hands on his round hips. He was a short, stout Bedouin whom Asad had never seen before in his life, yet the stranger seemed to know him. He said softly: "O my son, my son!"

Asad blinked owlishly. "Who is this man? I do not know him?"

"I am Farid Al Ghazzawi – your real father!"

Asad scowled in disbelief. "My real father is dead!"

"Thankfully, yes; my friend, Misfud Boulos has not seen what you've become! But I am here to stop your pranks, and your skulduggery!"

"I am no Bedouin!" Asad spat on the floor in disgust. "Old man – you smell of goat!"

"Do not insult me in front of Allah!" His father leaned down and slapped Asad's face. "You should treat Bedu's with ancestral honour! Know that we are fierce, proud people." He indicated the fifteen or so Bedouin men who were now grouped around him, their rifles hanging in relaxed fashion from their hands. "These are my people – the salt of the earth! But I am not proud of what you have become, you criminal!"

Asad sneered, forgetting his manners. "How could you, a fat little man of no repute, be my father?

I am a Boulos!"

"Only by name. By birth you are my son, born in a sand dune in the desert not so very far from here, where your lovely mother – Allah bless her – died in my arms after a terrible childbirth! She'd travelled to the desert to find me, wanting to tell her truth – that I was your real father, not Misfud! When I heard she was looking for me I ran to meet her, but reached her almost too late!"

"I was told my mother died in a hospital."

"Her body was taken to one after the birth. But septicaemia had set in and we couldn't save her. I left you with Misfud Boulos to bring up."

"You didn't want me then?" Asad smirked.

"Boulos thought you were his son. I let him think that... If I had bought you up as Bedu, I wonder if you would have turned out differently? We shall never know, for I have come here to ki –"

"Ghazzawi!" Came in a warning voice from Karl. "The man is injured; that should be enough justice! He is to be expedited for crimes in England as well as here!"

The old Bedouin faced Karl fiercely. "I must do this, don't you understand? He is no son of mine!" He had drawn a dagger from his robe and raised it over Asad's startled face.

They had forgotten the women, now Serena found her voice. She swiftly walked past the group of Bedouin's with guns, as if they were tormenting mosquito's to be brushed away with the hand, and spoke with venom to Al Ghazzawi.

"That's right! Kill the bastard – mutilate him!"

"Madam, it shall be done!" The old Bedouin raised his dagger and real fear swam in Asad's eyes.

He clutched Karl's leg and pleaded: "Don't let him do this, Englishman! I do not want to die!"

Karl put a hand on Al Ghazzawi's knife arm and held it firmly: "Drop the drama, my friend! I'll take it from here! Your son is responsible for kidnapping, extortion, amassing priceless, illegal antiquities, and selling youngsters into the slave trade – and murder! The two Arabs who left earlier, we have them; they are kingpins in the slave trade. Your men have caught them, and they should be congratulated. We could never have done this without your help and commitment to our cause."

Al Ghazzawi glowered at him. "For all his sins he deserves to die by my hand! Am I not his true, biological father? An eye for an eye!"

Karl shook his head. "Sorry! I can't let you do that! The Abu Dhabi police are waiting outside, and I would not want you to be taken in charged with the murder of this miserable man! Your family and tribe needs your attention now, not your bastard son! Let our form of justice take care of him."

Al Ghazzawi thought heavily, then, slowly lowered his sharp weapon. He said, in a slightly tired voice: "I have witnessed a revelation tonight. It will be as you ask; I'll spare his life, and he'll have to face whatever harsh punishment is coming to him. He can rot in jail here, or in England. I disown him! He is no longer my son!"

Asad Boulos had recovered some of his aplomb. He sneered at Al Ghazzawi maliciously. "If you are my father, as you claim, you should have kept your lecherous hands off my mother! The authorities will be interested to hear of your illicit liaison with her, and I will speak with them about you!"

Al Ghazzawi glared back. "You scoundrel, do not dare to threaten me – you are not in a position to! In the eyes of the law you have committed worse crimes than I! With your track record of murder and mayhem, do you think anyone will seriously believe you? I will tell them you lie to save your wretched skin! And I – as a good citizen of the desert, will be believed – not you! Accept that you wicked devil! Remember – the penalty here for murderers is death!"

Asad gritted his teeth and hung his head, the fire dying from his sardonic eyes, realising he could not give out orders so easily now. He was trapped, and he knew it!

Serena lowered the tension a little by asking Karl curiously: "What about that man lying on the floor who got shot? You spoke to him as though you knew him! Is he another 'kingpin'?"

"Peta? No, he's from the Abu Dhabi police, one of their undercover men whom I've been negotiating with on my mobile."

"An undercover policeman! How wicked! Will he be okay?"

"Luckily, yes, seems only a surface wound; he'll be fine!"

Resiliently, Serena, using her charms, appraised Karl

admiringly, and spoke warmly to him: "You put on the performance of a lifetime! You had me fooled, too – and you saved us! Congratulations!"

He ignored her interested attempt to attract him, and answered smoothly: "Yes, Mrs Wright, and I congratulate you on your plan to kidnap your own daughter! You nearly got away with it! Fran – can you come over and read this woman her rights?"

Serena gasped and her face fell.

Leigh had heard what Karl said to her mother, and was looking dumbly at her as if she didn't know her any more. She looked thunderstruck, and for once, was silent.

Still in pain, rooted to the floor, Asad issued a sudden harsh laugh at Serena's disbelieving, tormented expression. He knew she hadn't expected to be caught out so soon, and her undisguised agony amused him!

She reddened at his cruel snigger, and cried: "It was another man's idea, but Asad planned it all!" Before anyone could stop her, she'd grabbed the dagger from the old Bedouin's hand and lunged furiously at her would-be lover with all her might, with vengeance in her determined eyes.

# SATURDAY. A DASH FOR FREEDOM?

Tanja was tense. She had no way of knowing if their abductors had weapons. They didn't seem to have anything on them when they'd bought the chairs into the box room. She didn't even know what kind of house they were in. From the front, it had looked like a standard, modern detached home standing in its own grounds, away from neighbours and prying eyes. She and Kimmi had been man-handled swiftly into this box room which lay adjacent to the hall, and she hadn't seen any more. She didn't even know where they were, but felt she had to do something! If they could escape they might be able to knock on a neighbour's door and ask to make an emergency phone call.

She glanced down at her pensive daughter, whose eyes were darting here and there, like a trapped butterfly whenever she heard sounds of movement.

Tanja knew that what she was going to do was dangerous for both of them. But she had to try! Like the child, she couldn't bear being in this cooped-up box room another second!

From somewhere outside the house, there came a sudden commotion, as if cats were fighting, although it didn't sound like cats! Then, as she listened hard, someone began knocking on the front door! Kimmi jumped, and they heard shouting, both inside, and outside the house.

It was bewildering. Tanja cursed being this side of the door, unable to see. What was happening?  Footsteps seemed to sound everywhere!

Kimmi was watching her mother expectantly, biting her lip.

A key was being inserted into the door lock; the door knob handle began to turn...

Heart in her mouth, feeling 'this was it', Tanja awkwardly hefted the chair to her chest, ready to defend her child...

# ABU DHABI. FALL FROM GLORY

Asad cried out: "NO! You she-devil!" He raised his bloody hands to ward off Serena's determined attack, and to protect his face.

Before Serena could act, men of Al Ghazzawi's clan, recognising her intent, quickly surrounded the furious woman, and one man, Farid Al Ghazzawi's eldest son, Akmer, sent the lethal dagger spinning from her hand in a high kick.

It clattered across the floor, where Fran, on her way to cite Serena her citizen's arrest, picked it up and gave it to Karl as demurely as if she was offering him a slab of cake.

Leigh turned earnestly to Karl. "Never mind these crooked buggers! Isn't it time my father was told I'm safe?"

"Our men in England are doing that at this very moment." Karl told her. "Are you sure you're all right?"

"I'm all in, but I'll survive! They tried to kidnap me before!"

Karl nodded.

"Daddy hasn't paid any ransom yet, has he?"

"Not yet; I'm about to contact him."

"Thank you." Leigh's eyes dropped to the cowed Asad Boulos. She said accusingly: "You weren't ever going to send me home, were you? You were going to take daddy's money as well as sell me, and get even more money, you pig! How could you?"

Her mother said: "Yes; that's exactly true! He was tricking me as well as you!" She had sobered since she'd been read her rights, and was standing docile in her silver high heels between two restraining Bedouin's.

Farid Al Ghazzawi also looked down at his son in deep disgust. "You are an iniquitous, insouciant, and rapacious man! You have been spared death by my hand. This country has a harsh law for rogues, I dread what punishment you will be given before you reach England! Personally, I would have stoned you – a dagger is too easy for an ungrateful wretch like you! I am glad you will be found guilty and punished, and put away for a long, long time! If you should ever become free, I, or my men will find you, capture you, and send you into the merciless desert without food or water, and you will die there, I promise! Yes, you will die there, and the vultures will eat your infernal miserable, greedy heart and body, and I will not grieve for you!"

Leigh glared at her mother. "How could you get mixed up with him!" She indicated Asad, who was being helped upright, looking sorry for himself.

Serena answered tightly: "You know the score by now, darling! I've always been attracted to the wrong man!"

"Daddy was better than any of the others!"

"You're right, he was; my mistake and my misfortune." Serena gave a weary sigh.

Leigh warmed to her theme: "You call yourself a mother – you put me through hell and back because of your sexual cravings for the right man, and your greedy yearning for luxury and money! Well, it's put you somewhere now, hasn't it? I certainly won't attend your bloody trial! If the Abu Dhabi police get hold of you first, I hope they stone you!"

"Hell hath no fury –" recited Al Ghazzawi softly, to which quote Leigh burst into tears.

Fran moved over to her and held the sobbing girl in her arms. "It's okay, Leigh, it's over. You'll soon see your dad again!"

Through stormy tears Leigh stared at Fran in wonder. "You're so different from the timid little thing I knew! How come?"

"I'm a trained police Operative from an obscure branch of the CIUSO – like Karl. We were both ordered to watch you last night, but do nothing, except follow you. Your dad thought Karl was working for him."

"You mean – dad didn't know Karl was –?"

"No, your dad thought Karl was a minder – not part of our special police group."

"So it was a set-up with your organisation? I was the pawn?"

"Only so that we could catch Boulos in the act of either selling you, or demanding ransom money." Karl explained. He had rejoined the girls, having made sure the injured Peta was taken out of the Penthouse on a stretcher, at last. "It was a gambit – but it worked, thank God! Now we have evidence! You're witnesses, you saw what happened, and Peta was wired to catch most of what was said before he was shot!"

Al Ghazzawi mumbled something; Karl asked: "What's that?"

"My confession of fatherhood to my thug of a useless-son! Was that recorded?"

"It will be wiped! Peta will make sure of that! Don't worry!"

Reassured, Al Ghazzawi nodded his understanding.

"You really had it all planned, didn't you?" Leigh looked wonderingly at Fran and Karl. "So you two knew each other all the time, and I didn't suss it?"

"Yes!" They both chorused together, and a ghost of a smile touched Leigh's lips. Then, she frowned:

"Thinking about this now its all over – you're sods! Why did you let them do this to me?"

Karl answered her, hoping it would reassure: "We knew Boulos was going through with his plans: having you taken here was one way we could prove what Boulos was up to! Without absolute proof the Abu Dhabi police were powerless to intervene in his pseudo-rich life. He would have caused them grief with crooked lawyers trying to get him off the hook!"

"If he had so much money, why did he want daddy's?"

Karl shrugged. "He was that type of man! Never satisfied with what he had – greedily wanting more! Hoarding other people's money gave him power!"

"Yeah, he was a greedy slob!" Leigh agreed. She sobered, grimacing a little. "Like the first gang, you must have followed me to Mink's as well! You had a nerve! It was a damn cheek using me for your own ends! Like, I've sweated so much fear and distress living through this reality, it's changed me! I want to be something more than just an upper-class débutante now, and live and work how I want too, and I damn well will!"

She turned to the silent Fran. "I'm so glad you were with me, Fran! I would have screamed myself silly if there'd been no-one else with me! You seemed so calm and matter-of-fact for someone who's only eighteen; how old are you really?"

"I'm actually twenty!"

"Twenty? Yet you could handle a gun! How wild is that! But, something I don't understand... How did Karl know how to find us in Abu Dhabi, let alone where we were first taken to?"

Fran grinned. "I had a tracking device tucked into my bra at the start of all this! Karl followed us easily to that old cottage the gang dumped us in! Later, with my tracker no longer working for long-distance plane jetting, acting on verified information he received from CIUSO, Karl took off for the Emirates to find us – he had a shrewd idea where we were! You see Leigh, we were expecting something to happen last night! And when they took you, I was ready to jump forward and give them the opportunity to snatch me as well! It worked!"

"Thank God for that! Jesus, what a day! It's been so scary and fantastic! I feel like a balloon that's going to burst!"

The two girls hugged each other again.

"Fran? When we get back home, will you still be my friend? I want so much to get a job like you did! I'll be doing something worthwhile then!"

"Of course I will, Leigh! But my job was just an undercover story told for my parent's sake, so they wouldn't be too alarmed at what I was really doing! Don't worry, I'll help you look for a proper job when we get back, and after I've sorted this mess out with Karl!"

Leigh noticed the hapless Asad and her mother being

led away by the Bedouin's, to be handed over to police custody for the time being. "I can understand what made her do it. She was always after more money – like that conceited lover of hers! But why use me like that? I'll never forgive her for it! Some mother, huh?"

"Leigh?" Karl had been on his mobile. He handed it to her. "I've got someone here who badly needs to speak with you!"

"Dad!" Leigh's tired eyes lit up like a beacon. "Oh, at last! My dad!"

# LONDON. REVELATIONS

The doorbell rang at Paul Wright's house. He supposed it to be Ben Elliston and he opened his
front door to let the MP in.

A man with a mop of white hair, in shirt sleeves without his tie, and with his suit jacket flung casually over his shoulder was standing on the doorstep.

Paul vaguely recognised him.

"It's er, is it John Denby?"

"Yes. Hallo Mr Wright. I was passing, and I wondered if you'd heard anything more from the kidnappers?"

Paul blanched. "How d'you know –?"

"I'm a friend of Ben Elliston. He rung me and told me of your troubles. He was very concerned for you!"

Paul looked thunderstruck. "Ben had no right to do that!"

"I think he thought he was helping you! Has your daughter been kidnapped?"

"It's no concern of yours."

"I'm a policeman, Mr Wright. I've seen you down the club and I popped by on the off-chance, to
try and help you. Please let me!"

Paul hesitated. The man seemed genuine enough. He opened the front door wider. "You'd best come in. Call me Paul."

"Thanks, and call me John."

Paul led John to a dishevelled kitchen.

"Sorry about the mess. I've had a lot of paperwork to sort out! Would you like some whiskey?"

He indicated a half-full bottle.

"Yes, please. Thanks."

Paul reached up and took out a cut-glass crystal from

an overhead cabinet, and poured John out a generous measure.

"Cheers." They toasted each other in good malt whiskey. John cleared his throat.

"Have you heard anything yet, Paul?"

"Nope. But I'm paying the ransom. I want my daughter back safe and sound!"

"Another girl was kidnapped along with your daughter, I understand?"

"Yes, some other girl."

"I've had her parent's in my office. They are very worried about her."

"I suppose they are. I'm worried sick about Leigh! I'm surprised my hair hasn't turned grey!"

"When do you pay the ransom?"

"Tonight or tomorrow. In the evening."

"How?"

"By wire transfer, to an off-shore account. I'll be sent the details soon!"

"Would you like me to be here, to help you!"

"I've been told: 'no police'."

"Who by?"

"A man I hired to watch over my daughter's welfare – look, John, I appreciate your concern, but I must do this on my own!"

"I come as a friend, not as a copper!"

"I-I thank you for that, but you were asking me questions like one!"

"Sorry! Can't shake off the uniform!" They both smiled wanly.

The doorbell rang again.

"That's probably Ben. I'm expecting him."

It was Ben. He stopped short in the kitchen doorway when he saw John sitting there. "Hallo John! What's happening, Paul? Is Leigh okay still?"

John said to Ben. "I'm not here in my official capacity."

"Ah, I see..." Ben seemed ill at ease with John there. He turned to Paul who was pouring him some whiskey, and asked nervously: "Have you heard anything yet?"

"Only about the ransom sum. I heard Leigh's voice over the wire; she sounded so scared and panic-stricken, my poor girl!"

Ben murmured: "Their bastards, aren't they? How are you coping, Paul?"

Then, the doorbell rang for the third time!

Paul looked puzzled, but went to answer it, leaving Ben to exclaim: "Quite a party here tonight!  Wonder who it is?"

Two robust-looking men wearing suits despite the London heat, entered the kitchen, Paul following them. He said to John: "I've seen these men's credentials: their CIUSO Operatives!"

John looked nonplussed. "What are they doing here?"

One of the men walked up to him. "You're Denby, aren't you? You shouldn't be here..."

"I didn't come in my working capacity," John tried to explain, "I came as a friend! We all go to the same club and know one another!"

The newcomers appeared unconvinced. Paul looked puzzled, John a little guilty, and Ben still appeared uneasy.

One of the men said: "We're from Criminal Intelligence Unit Special Ops. We're here to see fair play done."

"In what way?" Asked John.

But the men wouldn't say.

Paul spoke stonily: "I didn't want the police involved – special ops or not."

"I'm Dan Hollbrook, sir, and this is Pat Smythe. We came to make your acquaintance, and to say, with your permission, that we'll hang around for the money transfer."

"You seem to know a lot about it!" Paul was staring hard at John, who dropped his eyes from the other man's accusing gaze. To his surprise, Dan Hollbrook said: "We've been monitoring this situation for some time, prior to your daughter's first kidnap. We know a lot about the man who has her –"

"Who is he?" Demanded Paul hotly. "I'd like to wring his bloody neck!"

"All told in good time, sir. Let's just say that you should hear soon, from an acquaintance you know. We hope its good news."

At that moment the kitchen phone rang. Paul pounced on it. "Yes?"

"Paul – OK? This is Silverman... We have your daughter – she's safe and well. I'll hand you over!"

Then he heard Leigh's elevated, relieved voice: "Dad? Oh, at last! My dad!"

"Leigh! You all right, sweetheart?" Sudden tears were running down Paul's weary face. He didn't bother to wipe them away. His worried features looked hard and drawn in the low glow of the discreet bespoke kitchen lights, but he was smiling now. "Thank God you're safe! I prayed and prayed you'd be all right!"

"Yes, yes, I'm tired, but fine. It's been very scary! I'll tell you all about it when I see you! Daddy – Karl wants a word with a man called Dan Hollbrook? Is he there? Oh, I love you Daddy!"

"I love you too gorgeous! Hold on, I'll pass you over to him!" Paul beckoned to the Special Ops man, who took the receiver quickly and spoke into it. After several minutes of animated speech, he hung up. He nodded to his companion, who approached Ben Elliston, and said: "Would you come with me, sir? You're under arrest!"

Ben spluttered: "W-what for?"

"For conspiracy to kidnap Leigh Wright!"

Paul looked thunderstruck. "Ben! What is this? I don't understand!"

"Ben Elliston helped in this little caper!" Dan Hollbrook explained to an astonished Paul and John.

"That's not true! I'm innocent!" Shouted Ben.

Hollbrook turned to him. "You associated for a couple

of years with Asad Boulos, and have been in touch with him, helping him to plan this operation! You also wanted a share of Paul Wright's income! You have been named by Asad Boulos and Serena Wright as a member of this kidnap organisation –"

"Serena? Did you say Serena? What the hell has she got to do with this?" Paul could hardly believe his ears. He sat heavily on a kitchen chair, looking exhausted. "I'm going mad!"

John got up and poured Paul another whiskey.

"Is this your ex-wife their talking about?" He asked.

"Yes. I can't believe it....! Serena? Involved with Leigh's kidnappers? It's too much to take in!"

The older man patted him in a fatherly way on the back.

"And now Ben? You're saying he's a criminal?"

Hollbrook's colleague had finished reciting Elliston's charge, he was now handcuffed, hotly denying his part in the proceedings.

Paul frowned. "Surely there's been some mistake?"

"Sorry, sir. We have it straight from the horses mouth; Mr Elliston is implicated in both kidnap attempts. An Arab millionaire named Boulos masterminded it, and Elliston helped from his end.   We have recent tapped phone reports of their overseas conversation, several calls to Abu Dhabi, made yesterday, at different times!"

"Eh? You had the cheek to tap my phone? You had no right!" Elliston squealed, red-faced.

"We've been watching you for some time, Mr Elliston!"

"Bloody hell! I'll have words with the PM over privacy issues on this!"

Hollbrook said firmly: "It won't wash – with the PM or no on your side – you can't get out of this Mr Elliston! We know you've cooperated with Boulos since 2015, when you first met him at an International Gala Evening in Abu Dhabi! Since then you've conducted a lot of dubious business with him – which we can trace back to your off-shore account!"

"Christ – Ben!" Paul Wright looked startled at this damning revelation.

A sullen Ben had gone quiet at the Operatives unshakable words, and John took the opportunity to ask Elliston as he was on the point of being led away: "Why did you try to involve me in this?"

Elliston shrugged, but didn't reply.

"Probably to muddy the waters, sir." Hollbrook replied earnestly, as his colleague ushered the crushed, handcuffed MP towards Paul's front door. "He reckoned to keep the police busy over this kidnap affair – get all the divisions in a tizzy with each other to throw the scent off him! The Met don't have data on Boulos yet, but we do! Secretly, Mr Elliston's kept a low profile about his Abu Dhabi connections, which we also know about; it's been a planned operation by us to get evidence on Asad Boulos without Elliston realising it. Unfortunately, he found out about us from DCI John Denton. CIUSO didn't want any leaks, or investigations made by the Met to the Abu Dhabi police in case Boulos caught a whiff of it!" Hollbrook glanced over at John as he spoke, who fidgeted in his chair.

"I see, thank you for explaining all this!" Paul glared accusingly at Elliston. "How could you do this to me, Ben?"

Elliston shrugged. He murmured: "You had the money! I had the means! Serena would have ensured your daughter got back safely – so, where's the panic?"

"I don't take this lightly, you bastard!"

"It didn't happen like that!" Hollbrook chimed in. All the men turned their attention back to him expectantly.

"What do you mean?" Paul asked.

Hollbrook spoke again to Paul. "We now know that Boulos had plans to sell your daughter off to the highest bidder who claimed her; he'd organised a secret meeting of slave traders to meet at his apartment, to buy off the girls. Then, he was going to ask you to send off your money to his off-shore account and add it to his ill-gotten gains, without returning you're daughter!"

"Christ – I can't believe this! It's so horrendous! When did you hear all this?"

"Just now, when I spoke on the phone, to one of our colleagues in Abu Dhabi, who witnessed it!"

Paul noticed the sudden surprise in Ben Elliston's shocked features. He couldn't resist asking, spitefully: "Why the long face, Ben? It's not funny being held by the law, is it? Was this devil friend of yours two-timing you as well? Didn't you guess what a cunning shit he was?"

"God, no! He told me he'd return Leigh, via Serena, once he'd got your money! Paul – I had no idea he'd attempt this awful subterfuge! The man is a maniac, a rotten scoundrel! I wish now I hadn't been roped into his crazy schemes! It seemed a golden opportunity at the time..!"

"What have I ever done to you, you unbelievable scheming tyke?" Paul grated out, his normally placid grey eyes staring fiercely at the disillusioned MP.

Elliston shrugged. He wouldn't meet Paul's demanding gaze.

Hollbrook broke the tension, turning back to Paul. "As said before, we knew about the first kidnap attempt. Knowing our suspects profile, we made plans in case he should try again, and CIUSO had our best Arab-speaking Operative put on the job, sending him out to the Emirates!"

Paul shook his head, trying to take this information in. He still looked angry and agitated. "So, who is the man you put on the job? I'd like to thank him, for finding my daughter!"

"His name is Karl Silverman!"

"But, that's who I –!"

"We know!"

"I can't take this in! Silverman followed the girls to Abu Dhabi to help me get my daughter back, I thought! Now you say Karl Silverman is really an Operative of yours, working for CIUSO? I don't get it – he was recommended to me by a friend of Ben Elliston's! I hired him to work for me!"

"That is so... But your agreement with Silverman is null and void as of now! Elliston didn't know that Silverman worked for us either! We had to keep Silverman's mission hush-hush from the Met; we didn't want crossed-wires with zealous coppers swarming on our patch, alerting Elliston! This was classed as an international incident between us and the Abu Dhabi police – who cooperated with us!" Hollbrook glanced meaningfully again at John, who looked suitably embarrassed this time.

Paul looked as if there was still thunder brewing in his mind. He was thinking of this situation, and of his daughter's startling abduction agony. He asked, Hollbrook, who was about to take his leave:

"I get the feeling..., was this some kind of set-up by your people? Karl Silverman told me he couldn't intervene and stop Leigh being taken, he let her shoot off to her fate without, apparently, interfering with this kidnap operation! Silverman said: he wouldn't allow any harm to come to Leigh – yet this whole, 'organised' approach by you lot, and him, is sneaky, to say the least! I demand from your firm, some kind of compensation for what we both have suffered in the last 24 hours!"

Hollbrow gave Paul a tight smile, and nodded comfortingly. "On behalf of the CIUSO I'm extremely sorry for what you and your daughter have been exposed to! As you know we are a special, elite organisation. We had to act how we thought best, sir. Boulos had made further secondary plans to abduct your daughter to Abu Dhabi, and this gave us the chance to seize him and his cronies for several crimes we knew he had committed in England, but couldn't prove! I venture to add – isn't having your daughter home, safe and well, compensation enough? If you are still unhappy about our methods, I'll speak to our Chief Operative and have him call you!"

"It's not good enough! Leigh could have been killed – anything could have happened to her, man!"

"Both Silverman and the other kidnapped Operative –

Fran Tompkins, were in the same room as your daughter. Our special Operative kept his promise that no harm would come to Ms Wright! He acted when the time was right and had the whole show under control within minutes! Leigh was perfectly safe in Silverman's hands – and we got our man, thanks to you and your daughter!"

Paul shrugged, giving in, suddenly feeling his age. "I suppose... It doesn't matter! Leigh's safe, that's the main thing! God! What a day this is! When will I get my daughter home?"

"It will be a few hours, but I can assure you, she's on her way! Goodbye, sir. You won't have to make the money transaction now! And you don't have to see us out!" Hollbrook prepared to leave with his non-speaking comrade and their subdued charge.

"Thank heavens for that! I've had enough shocks for one day!" And Paul drained his whiskey glass in one go, hearing his unexpected visitors departing via the front door.

He said to John: "Silverman told me my daughter was in the Emirates somewhere, and Serena flew out there two years ago... I hadn't connected it up before now, and I just can't understand why my ex-wife should connive to kidnap her own flesh and blood – there's a man in it somewhere!"

John nodded. "This Boulos thug probably. Ben Elliston must have introduced her to him! If it's any consolation, Paul, in my book, women do some funny things for love!"

"You're right there! Serena was a first class bitch, and put her with wicked men, she was putty in their hands."

"Yeah, Boulos sounds a right schemer! He must have been mad, to think he'd get away with his kidnap idea!"

"Absolutely, yes – I nearly lost my daughter and my money, but Karl Silverman did save my girl – as he promised! Despite him not stopping Leigh's kidnap, as he was paid to do!"

John patted Paul on the back as he passed him. "Silverman sounds like a cool Operative who takes a lot of risks! Well, I must go. I'm glad you'll be getting your daughter back soon. Thanks for the whiskey! Good afternoon!"

"Yes, thanks for trying to help. I'll see you around at the club! Goodbye!"

# LONDON. UNEXPECTED NEWS

Nigel was peering out of the front lounge window curtain. He said: "I don't want to worry you, dear, it's a bit late in the afternoon for visitors..., but a couple of iffy-looking gents are walking down our garden path!"

"Oh, no, let's see!" Mandy flew to the window and stared out. "Who could they be?"

"I'll go and find out. You wait here!"

Nigel left a worried Mandy holding on to the back of her dining chair. From where she stood she heard one of the men standing on the doorstep outside mumble enquiringly: "Are you Mr. Nigel Tompkins?"

Apparently, Nigel must have let them in, for they were entering her lounge, two grim-looking men whom she'd never seen before.

Her heart dropped like a stone. "It's about Fran, isn't it? Whatever has happened to her, do you know?"

"Good evening. Mrs Mandy Tompkins, isn't it? Would you care to sit down?"

She sat, abruptly, onto the chair, staring up at the men with frightened, worried eyes.

"Fran....?"

"We're agents from the Criminal Intelligence Unit Special Ops."

Nigel and Mandy both looked puzzled. "Who are Special Ops?" Nigel asked.

"A trained, elite Police Unit, set up to catch resilient criminals!"

"But, you've come about Fran, haven't you?" Mandy burst out. "What has she done for heaven's sake, that you pay us a visit?"

"We've come to say that you're daughter, Fran, has

been working for us for over a year now. But she wasn't allowed to tell you this!"

Startled, Nigel began: "Her job at the charity shop, you mean it never –?"

"Was? No. Sorry for the deception!"

"I don't care where she worked! Just tell me if she's OK, please!" Moaned Mandy, in despair, wringing her hands.

"Sorry, Mrs Tompkins, I was just going to. No, Fran is fine. She's completed a very tricky job for us, but she's all right – you'll be able to speak to her soon, when she flies back!"

"Why, wherever has she been?" Nigel asked as he grabbed his wife's hand in jubilation.

"Oh, she's okay! Thank God!" Mandy began to cry.

The man from Special Ops grinned. "She's been jet-setting! She'll tell you a little about it when she sees you. But she can only say so much because of the Official Secrets Act"

"When will that be?" Nigel asked realising that his wife was too overcome to speak properly yet.

"Tomorrow afternoon sometime – Heathrow. She's just got a few formalities to complete on the job she was doing for us! Then she'll be off, back to London!"

"We'll be there to meet her," beamed Nigel. "Won't we, dear?"

"Oh, God, yes!" Mandy had found her voice. Her lined face looked radiant. "We'll definitely welcome her home! Thank-you! Thank-you, for telling us such wonderful news! We were so worried about her!"

# ABU DHABI. A DESERT CELEBRATION!

The feasting and celebrations had gone on well into the night. Karl had enjoyed the Bedouin's offering of a sumptuous meal again – a mixture of frozen meat and vegetables bought that day into camp by the easy-going camels. There were hard and soft cheeses, and a variety of mango's, melons and dates, washed down with very sweet soft drinks out of a can. The Bedouin's, he decided happily, knew how to live under the stars of the desert! It might not be the most modern example of life, yet he succumbed thoroughly to its sirens song, and drank in its simple wonders like a man seduced by strong wine.

Having guests beside him brought out the best in Farid Al Ghazzawi's temperament. As host, he called for the whole clan to join him beside the large camp fire, and his people came, proud of him, pleased with what he'd accomplished that night with Karl's planned ghazwas, hearing that their unshakable leader had unhesitatingly severed the ties from his bastard son at last, and had told his truth.

Al Ghazzawi, lastly, tasted his food, still toasting Karl. He had put aside any bitter memories that Asad Boulos may have left him with, and was hell bent on merry-making with his people around him. And he was enjoying Derrick's easy company. To Dickie he had spoken of his lengthy, hard life wandering the desert, and Dickie had told him of his past adventures in the war, and of his retirement, enjoying life back home, living fairly near his son and family.

Derrick concluded to the amiable Bedouin: "I'm glad you and your men and Karl made it back safely tonight. Karl has told me all about your ghazwas – I'm still amazed over the second kidnap girl hiding under a false persona, acting scared about what happened to her! And Karl – dressing up as a rich camel-racer, completely pulling the wool over his enemy's eyes! How plucky is that?

It's a pity I missed some of the excitement. But probably best that I did!"

Understanding this, Al Ghazzawi patted Derrick on the back.

"You would have found it very unexciting. My men blew in the door and rushed in with their rifles. Our ghazwas was over within minutes, and Karl had it all under control! I wandered in when the time was right and berated my bastard son, intending harm to him, but Karl stopped me! He knew what he was doing... He is an inspiring, brave young man – as you war-time warriors were!"

"Back in the forties we men had to be brave, we did what we were trained for, scrambling to defend our country from Hitler's incendiary bombs!"

"Then I toast you, for your bravery under murderous enemy fire! Have some more wine..!"

"I think I've had enough! I'm almost dropping off to sleep! I thought Muslims weren't supposed to drink?"

"Ah, but this is a celebration, my friend! I shall pray and repent towards Allah tomorrow!"

Derrick laughed, then yawned loudly, and the old Bedouin patted him kindly on his thin, bowed back again.

"Ha, Dickie! Is it past your bed-time?" Al Ghazzawi joked.

"It's the wine..., I haven't drunk so much in a long time! I'm tipsy!"

"You are welcome to sleep here – even to stay here until your visa runs out. I shall arrange it!"

"That is kind of you, but I think Karl's man, Rachid, is coming to collect me."

"It has been a long day for you, my friend! You are not so used to this weather as I am!"

"Yes, it has been hot and tiring, but I wouldn't have missed it for the world! Thanks for having me!"

"It has been my pleasure! You are still welcome to stay here; I do not want to lose a good friend so soon."

"I have to pack for home tomorrow."

"Then I shall miss you. We must keep in touch."

"I would like that."

Al Ghazzawi's eyes had been roaming around the camp-fire, now he nudged Derrick's arm.

"Something tells me that my only daughter is smitten with Karl – look at her! Her eyes have followed him everywhere since he got back!"

Derrick saw. He said: "I think Karl might stay; he seems 'smitten' as well, don't you think?"

"Yes. Yes. Perhaps I should get them together, although I do not want them to get into trouble with the authorities! Watch this!"

Generously, he turned to a surprised Karl and stated: "My eldest daughter, Leda, is making sheep's eyes at you, do you lust after her as well, I wonder?"

Karl flashed Leda a quick glance from where she was sitting with the other Bedouin women, chatting animatedly. "Believe me, I am tempted..."

"Then what stops you? Our laws must seem harsh and strict to an Englishman, used to modern world standards! It is hard for women here to find true love. They are curtailed by our eastern laws; trying to keep Islamic faith, and worrying about their punishment if they don't! Many resist marrying, although the government encourage them to! These women do not want to be held as chattel's under their husband's domination, to be subservient, especially if he should hit her! Sadly, that happens! Today's modern woman wants better reforms! But my daughter is her own woman in my eyes! She is freer to choose who she wishes to be with, than others can! We men of the desert are not so old fashioned in our ways as we used to be, and Leda admires you! Isn't that enough?"

"I thought I might need to ask your permission to court her!"

Al Ghazzawi chuckled: "Such an old-fashioned word

coming from the lips of a modern man! But I give my permission freely! Know that you are always welcome here, although a union between you both could bring trouble! You see what a fatalist I am! Now go – go! Be with Leda as your heart desires it! We are not being watched – only the desert sees things it shouldn't!" He grabbed Karl's hand and held it to his chest. The two men embraced in a great tide of friendship under the glowing stars of the Milky Way.

Karl stood up. He said to the drowsy Derrick, who had been listening sLeighpily to their exchange: "I'm going for a walk with Leda. Rachid should be here for you soon. Goodbye for now, my friend. We'll meet again, and I'll be in touch!"

Derrick coughed, to hide his emotion. The pair gallantly shook hands, and Karl gave him a warm clap on the back, as he passed him.

Leda watched him approach her and she smiled brilliantly at him as she stood up, guessing rightly, that the embrace between her father and Karl had been made because of her.

She hastened over to Derrick and placed a friendly hand on his blanketed shoulder. She seemed to smell of a desert perfume and he had to ask her what it was called.

"I call it 'Queen of heaven'!" She told him with a gamine smile. "I made it myself from essential oils; rose, vanilla, bergamot and musk."

"Really? So clever of you! You are a queen, m'dear!"

"Thank you! I shall blow you a kiss goodbye for that! Return to us soon! You will be very welcome here."

Just then Rachid turned up, and Karl helped Derrick to his feet. The two men embraced carefully, whilst Al Ghazzawi took hold of the Derrick's arm and led him gently and proudly to Rachid's 'old jalopy', after handing him back his stick.

Derrick went to give back the richly embroidered cloak he'd borrowed to sit in front of the fire, his pale face lighting up with a soft, trusting smile at his erstwhile new

Bedouin friend, but

AL Ghazzawi stopped him. "Keep it, Dickie, with my compliments. May it keep you warm all the way home!"

"Thank you so much! I have really enjoyed today!" With a little help, Derrick arranged himself in Rachid's rough old car seat, a very happy man, and waved goodbye to everyone.

After he had gone, leaving a well of silence behind him at his departure – only the crackling fire could be heard for a moment, and as Karl stood by the large glowing camp fire he noticed Leda was now wearing an embroidered thick golden cloak around her blue dress, for the desert air was chill, and she gave Karl a cloak also, saying: "It will be cold away from the fire, habibi."

He took the cloak gratefully, not having packed a suitable coat or jumper. It was definitely getting chilly – he had goosebumps! In the desert the heat fell away to about only 4 or 5 degrees at night – and could go even lower, to minus 3 degrees in cooler weather months!

"You called me 'habibi'. Perhaps you don't realise that I know what it means?"

She had the grace to blush, although, in the darkness as they turned away from the fire, he did not notice this. "Then you'll know it means 'beloved'. Habibi means 'my love'."

Karl, briefly, thought again of his firm, airy words to Tanja. That episode seemed a world away from this moment. Coming out here, to this stimulating, exotic desert land had changed something in him; he seemed somehow ready for this change, even though he felt sad and guilty over the way he'd handled Tanja's and Kimmi's predicament, and had, presumably, led Tanja to think he meant something to her.

Easily, he heard himself ask: "And am I...your love?"

"You could be."

Acceptance was everything, he held back any caution and dived in, remembering what Al Ghazzawi had earnestly told him earlier. "Then I would like to be."

She was about to speak, but his mobile rang. Karl groaned. "Sorry! S'cuse me?"

He pulled it from his back pocket quickly, anxiously wondering if the CIUSO men had a better report on Tanja and Kimmi's whereabouts.

"Hi, Drake! Got any good news for me?"

A vibrant woman's voice answered him: "Hallo! Is that you, Karl?" He recognised it, and his features lit up.

"Tanja! Thank God – I've been so worried! Are you and Kimmi okay? Where are you? How did you get this number?"

He heard her laugh breathlessly, as if she'd been running. "No one's told me where we are yet! Your guys from CIUSO have just rescued us! They tracked us down and arrested the two men who took us! One of them lent me his mobile, as I badly wanted to contact you! He told me you were abroad, and I begged him for this number! He was reluctant at first, as it was a very private number! But I got my way in the end!"

Karl glanced at Leda. She was watching him a little warily, trying not to look too interested in his conversation...

"You nearly always do – bar one memorable occasion I could mention! Are you sure you're both all right?"

"Yeah, we were a bit frightened, but we weren't harmed. The men who grabbed us thought you were living with us! I put them right, though they didn't believe me! They locked us in some kind of box room. They bought us some wooden chairs to sit and eat on... I was going to try and force our way out, using one of the chairs as a battering ram! But I was unsure of attacking them – they were big guys to muck about with! Luckily, when the door did open, it was to find your men standing there, ready to rush in! I never felt so relieved in my life! It was perfect timing! We're both so glad to be out! And – Karl?"

"What, my lovely?"

"I'm sorry about what I said to you! It was rotten of me to treat you like I did! When you get back to London, I want your blessing!"

"Whatever for? You know I'm very fond of you and Kimmi! You don't have to ask me for a pardon! Why a blessing?"

"Because we're both okay now – and safe, and I've decided to marry Kostas – he proposed to me before you left! It was why I was so pissed off with you, but you told me how you really felt about us, and I should have accepted it, instead of getting so steamed up! My temper from the old days came out. Am I forgiven?"

"Tanja – of course you are! It's a weight off my mind to know you're both safe! I wanted to come back to help find the pair of you! But I had to stay here and finish this job – it was so hard – I couldn't join in the search!"

"I believe you! Where is 'here'"

"I'm in the Emirates. My mission is nearly complete, but I have a lot of loose ends to tie up before I arrive back in Britain. You might have to wait for that blessing, but I'll give you it now, if you like! Congratulations, Tanja! I wish you every happiness!"

"Thanks, Karl! I shall miss you! You've been a good friend to both of us! I realise that now!"

"Okay, I understand...see you sometime! Bye for now, Tanja! Give my love to Kimmi! I'm so glad she's all right!"

He switched off, turning to Leda, smiling happily.

"Good news?" She asked, doe-eyed, trying not to show her innate curiosity.

"Very! A friend in England was in a spot of trouble! But she's fine now! She's planning to get married – to my surprise, which has made me feel less upset! I'm glad for her!"

"You look pleased!"

"Yeah! Tanja deserves to be happy at last! She's had a rough past!"

"Who is this Tanja? A girlfriend of yours? It sounds like she means a lot to you!" Leda sounded a little suspicious. She was feeling her way carefully, not sure if Karl would welcome her slightly jealous questioning.

"We're just good friends! Tanja disowned me for awhile; she had issues with me, and came over so fiery that I had to refuse her wishes! But I'm really pleased she and her daughter are safe now – they've been like family to me! Remind me to tell you about it some time. Er, what were you going to say before we were interrupted?"

Leda considered, shelving her curiosity for the moment, and said, slowly and seriously: "Somehow you have crept into my heart. So I accept you! You are a brave, forward-thinking man, and I like that, and respect you for it."

"That's strong praise! You Bedouin women are not afraid to say what you think! I seemed to have found a soul-mate! Plus a beautiful woman who appears to understand me – that's a real bonus!"

"I sense this also...it is kismet."

They smiled easily at each other.

In silence, they walked in the sand dunes, as close together as they dared, and as the noise from the camp-fire crowd faded, the cold, twinkly, starry night became their haven...

And ex squadron leader Derrick 'Dickie' Fairs, now being driven back to his hotel, sitting in Rachid's dusty old passenger seat wrapped in his thick cloak, smiled for the young couple's happiness. He was pleased it had ended well for them, but wondered what had happened to Karl's other lady friend. As Karl had said, he'd hear from him soon, and would be told about it!

Tomorrow, he would travel home, and his 'adventure' would be over, but what a story he would have to tell his son and daughter-in-law when he saw them!

Printed in Great Britain
by Amazon

39210858R10101